What's the Matter
Royston Knapper?

Gervase Phinn is a very proud father of four, a master of
storytelling, a teacher, freelance lecturer, author, poet, educational
consultant and visiting professor of education.

His first book, *The Other Side of the Dale*, was published
in 1998, followed by *Over Hill and Dale* and
It Takes One to Know One. This is his first book
of fiction for children.

Other books by Gervase Phinn

The Other Side of the Dale
Over Hill and Dale
It Takes One to Know One

Gervase Phinn

What's the Matter, Royston Knapper ?

Illustrated by Chris Fisher

For my children:
Richard, Matthew, Dominic and Elizabeth

Published by Child's Play (International) Ltd
Ashworth Road, Bridgemead, Swindon SN5 7YD

www.childs-play.com

Text copyright © Gervase Phinn 2001
Illustrations copyright © A. Twinn 2001
Printed in Croatia

ISBN 0-85953-883-4 paperback 0-85953-884-2 hardback

1 3 5 7 9 10 8 6 4 2

A catalogue reference for this book is available from the British Library

Contents

The Ghost of Gritstone Grange

Mr Masterson's nose was an inch from the boy's face. He spat out the words. "Every day you are sent to my room for one thing or another, aren't you, Royston Knapper?"

"Yes, Sir."

"Chattering in class!"

"Yes, Sir."

"Not doing your homework!"

"Yes, Sir."

"Poking your nose into other people's business!"

"Yes, Sir."

"Getting into scrapes!"

"Yes, Sir."

"Missing school!"

"Yes, Sir."

"The list goes on and on."

"Yes, Sir."

"Royston, will you stop repeating, 'Yes, Sir' in that silly tone of voice every time I take a breath!" snapped the headteacher. "You sound like a parrot."

"Yes, Sir."

Mr Masterson gave a great heaving sigh. "You spend more time in my room than you do in your classroom."

The boy shifted uneasily, gave a pathetic little cough and held his head down.

"And look at me when I'm speaking to you, young man," continued the headteacher, fixing him with a fierce glare.

The boy looked up. He opened his mouth to say something but when he saw the red and glowering face before him, he thought better of it.

"And every time you are sent to me, you have some wild and wonderful excuse, some incredible story, some far-fetched, fanciful reason, don't you?" Royston realised that Mr Masterson was not really expecting an answer. " 'I was just walking past the window and it sort of fell out!' 'The ferret was sick on my homework!' 'I thought we were on holiday that day!' 'A dog ran off with my sports kit!' 'It just came off in my hand!' All weird and wonderful excuses."

Royston gave a little nod of agreement but decided to keep his mouth firmly closed.

"If there's any trouble, you seem to be in the thick of it. Casualty and calamity, mishap and misfortune follow you around. And when you make one of your frequent visits to my office, it's always somebody else to blame, isn't it? Never you! Well, I am most interested to hear what you have to say for yourself about this latest reckless prank. What extraordinary tale have you concocted this time, I wonder?"

The boy took a deep breath, bit his bottom lip nervously and mustered up his most pitiful look but he remained silent. "Come on, Royston, out with it! What have you got to say for yourself?"

The boy braced his shoulders and gave another small cough before replying. "Nothing, Sir."

"Nothing, Sir," repeated Mr Masterson smiling. It was not a very pleasant smile. "Do my shell-like ears deceive me, Royston Knapper, or are you, for once in your life, lost for words?"

"I didn't mean it to hit him, Sir. It was a terrible mistake, a sort of unfortunate accident."

Mr Masterson's face ballooned with anger. "Didn't mean it to hit him!" he roared. "Didn't mean it to hit him! You threw a brick at him. What did you think would happen? How in heaven's name can it be a terrible mistake, a sort of unfortunate accident as you call it, when you deliberately hurled a brick at him?"

"Sir, it wasn't a brick, it was a pebble," said the boy quietly, looking at the headteacher with the most innocent of expressions. "And he moved."

Mr Masterson closed his eyes, shook his head dramatically and gave a great heaving sigh. "I am really not interested whether the missile you flung was a brick, a pebble, a boulder, a paving slab, the Rock of Gibraltar or a red-hot meteorite. It was you who threw the stone at the water bus, wasn't it? And it was you who nearly fractured

3

the driver's skull. You will no doubt remember the driver, who, according to you, was obviously to blame for moving! He was in my office for a good half hour complaining about you."

Royston noticed that Mr Masterson's chin wobbled when he shouted and that his eyes seemed to pop out. His long bald head was now red and shiny.

He recalled the incident when he had thrown the pebble at the Sprotborough water bus. How could he forget it? He had been down by the canal doing a spot of fishing near Greenwood Lock when the water bus, full of children, all gleaming and glistening in school uniform, had come spluttering by. He would not have moved from his position on the bank, but the noisy great boat had churned up all the water and disturbed the fish. The vessel had chugged noisily towards him, belching out smoke and creating the most enormous waves, just at the very moment when a great barrel-bodied pike had been about to take his bait. The fish, feeling the movement in the water, had sunk slowly back into the dark weeds at the bottom of the canal. Royston had tossed down his rod, jumped up and down furiously and had shouted out a few colourful words at the driver – a big, ugly, hairy man in shirt sleeves – who had replied: "You shouldn't be down here fishing anyway! You should be at school. I shall report you when I get to the next landing."

It had been a spur of the moment thing. Royston had picked up a pebble the size of a hen's egg and hurled it angrily at the boat. He thought it would land harmlessly with a plop in the water but, instead, it had shot in the direction of the driver and hit him with a loud crack on his forehead. And that's when all the trouble had started.

The wounded driver had shrieked, smacked his hand to his head, staggered and steered the boat towards the bank. Then, leaping ashore with the agility of an ape, he had grabbed Royston by the collar and shaken him until his teeth had rattled.

"I meant the pebble to make a bit of a splash in the water," he now explained feebly to the headteacher, who was edgily tapping his fingers on his desk. "I really didn't mean it to hit him on the head, Sir. Honest."

Mr Masterson gave him a long and blistering look. It was with some difficulty that he attempted to control his anger. "And what about the week before? I had to see you in my room yet again, this time for telling Noleen Midgely that the school doctor was drunk and using rusty needles to give the Rubella injections."

Royston remembered Noleen sitting there all wide-eyed and taking in his grisly story. "Once, the needle he was using snapped off in this girl's arm," he had told the terrified

5

girl, whilst pulling the most gruesome face imaginable, "and there was blood and broken needles everywhere!"

It had taken Mrs Gabbitas two hours, three huge mugs of hot chocolate, and a wet flannel to calm the distraught Noleen down.

"It was just a bit of fun, Sir," said the boy, prodding himself into a weak smile. "I didn't think she'd take me seriously."

"Like the week before that, I suppose? Just a bit of fun!" said the headteacher sourly. "I had Gillian Kershaw's mother in my room for a full hour complaining about you and she certainly did not see the amusing side, I can tell you that!"

Royston had been rummaging through a stack of boxes in his grandad's attic, looking for some postcards, when he had come upon a World War II gas mask. It had been in a battered brown cardboard case and smelt dusty and old. He had put it on and when he looked at himself in the mirror the

effect had been quite frightening: large, round, glassy eyes
set in thick black rubber and a long concertina-like snout,
which hung down with a khaki-coloured kind of bean tin on
the end. He had immediately seen its potential for mischief.
Later that afternoon he had waited outside the Christabel
Cathcart School of Dancing where Gillian took ballet
lessons. As she had tripped daintily down the steps, he had
leapt out of the shadows, his hood up and the ugly gas mask
covering his face, making the most awful growling and
grunting noises. He had never seen anybody move so fast.
Gillian was up those steps like a rabbit with its tail on fire.
She had fastened herself as tight as a tentacle around
Miss Cathcart's legs. It had taken ten minutes to peel her
off, like a strip of elastoplast, and even then Miss Cathcart
had not understood a word of what the hysterical girl was
saying: "It was horrible, horrible, Miss. It had round shining
eyes as big as footballs and a long rubbery snout, and it
made this awful growling noise!"

Mr Masterson was still rambling on. "Mr Draycott won't have you involved with any more school sports fixtures after the unpleasant affair at Cornfield School. The captain of their team is still seeing a doctor. You are also not attending any more school discos, after the incident with the fire extinguisher, which you claim miraculously jumped off the wall when you were passing. Mr Draycott has very nearly given up teaching because of you, Royston Knapper, and I have been having serious thoughts about it as well. Mr Draycott and I came into this profession to teach well-behaved, interested, hard-working pupils, not deal day after day with troublesome, disruptive, noisy children like you who cannot stay out of mischief. You attract trouble like a human magnet!"

"How is Mr Draycott, Sir?" asked Royston pleasantly.

"He won't be back at school until ... Never mind how Mr Draycott is! We are not here to discuss Mr Draycott's health. We are here to discuss what I am going to do with you, you silly boy! For your information, Mr Draycott is still in a state of shock and will be off school for the rest of the term, so Mrs Gabbitas will continue to take your class for the time being. When Mr Draycott does return, he has to take things easy and not get over-excited, and he has vowed, after your little escapade in Switzerland, that never again will he take children abroad."

The school trip to Switzerland had been great, especially the last night when Penelope Pringle had had hysterics.

Penelope Pringle was a small pixie-like girl with big eyes, and enormous, pink-framed spectacles that made her eyes look even bigger. She was best at everything in the class and she knew it. Her writing was always beautifully neat and imaginative, her number work predictably accurate, her careful and detailed art work superior to everyone else's efforts by far. She was also the best at sports and music. By contrast, Royston's English book looked as if a spider had emerged from an ink pot and crawled drunkenly across the page. Number work was not his favourite subject, he was not all that keen on Geography, or History, and he hated Science; his books had more crosses than gravestones in a cemetery. In Art, Royston invariably got more paint on himself than he did on the paper. He liked football but tended, such was his enthusiasm, to kick other pupils rather than the ball, hence the problem with the captain of Cornfield School football team. In singing, he sang so loudly and out of tune that he was told to mime because it put the others off. Royston did not like Penelope who he thought was the teacher's pet and a know-all, and Penelope disliked Royston who she found as irritating as an unscratched itch.

"There are trolls in Switzerland, you know," he had told Penelope casually at the breakfast table of the Hotel Untergrund where they had been staying on the school trip abroad. "Little, vicious, hunchbacked hairy dwarf-like creatures who creep into your bedroom at night and grab you while you're asleep."

"Go away, Royston Knapper," Penelope had replied with elaborate indifference. "I'm not interested in your ridiculous stories."

"They live hidden in the shadows under bridges in the day, but scuttle out when it's dark. Little hairy creatures they are, with sharp teeth and bristly beards."

"Don't be so stupid," Penelope had replied, helping herself to another piece of toast and looking haughtier than ever. "Do you think I was born yesterday?"

"It's true," Royston had persisted. "They're all wrinkled and gnarled and smelly, with sharp pointed teeth dripping with blood and claw-like feet and…"

"And you're out of your tiny little mind if you think I'd believe that. You might have frightened Noleen Midgely with your ridiculous story about drunken doctors, and Gillian Kershaw with your silly gas mask, and Frances Partington when you said the cable car was coming off the wire, but you won't frighten me." She had taken a big bite of her slice of toast.

"Has anybody ever told you, Pringly," Royston had said, screwing up his face as if sucking a lemon, "that you look just like a shark when you're eating?"

That night when the teachers were relaxing in the Alpine Bar, after an exhausting trip up Mount Pilatus in a creaking cable car full of screaming children, Royston had waited for Penelope at the door to her bedroom. "He's in there," he had whispered.

"Who is?"

"The troll, all hairy and smelly, and waiting to grab you."

"Oh, do go away!" Penelope had shouted, pushing past him. "You are so immature, Royston Knapper, do you know that?" Once inside her room she had stopped by the bed and had stared at a large round lump underneath the blankets.

She looked about as frightened as a charging bull.

"I told you," Royston had whispered from the door.

Penelope had stared for a moment at the mound before pulling back the sheet and blankets to reveal a pillow. "Oh very funny," she had said, a sarcastic grin on her face. "I'm really frightened of a pillow. Do you know something, Royston Knapper, you've got about as much sense as a stupid chimpanzee, and what's more, you look like one!" And with that she had slammed the door.

When Penelope had arrived at her room the next night, she had found the pillow pushed into a mound underneath the bedclothes. It had been there again the next night, and the next, and the next.

"If you don't stop going in my room, Royston Knapper, and messing up my bed, I'm telling Mr Draycott," Penelope had told him on the last day. "Nobody finds it the least bit funny, you know."

"How do you know it's me?" Royston had asked.

"Because nobody else is so childish and stupid," Penelope said, "and if you think you can scare me with your stories about trolls in people's beds, then you are out of your tiny little mind."

That night when she had arrived at her room, Penelope

had found the mound in her bed as usual. She had sighed and shaken her head, changed into her nightie, brushed her teeth, had a quick wash, turned off the light and climbed into bed. As she had reached down for the pillow something had moved next to her. Then a cold and clammy hand had grabbed her wrist and she had felt sharp bristles rub against her arm.

"Aaaaaahhh!" she had shrieked. "Aaaaaahhh! It's the troll!" She had shot out of her room and down the corridor. The next thing was the fire alarm ringing wildly, half-dressed people rushing down the stairs and Mr Draycott, minus his false teeth and dressed in a bright tartan dressing gown, trying to round up the pupils. Meanwhile, Royston had crept from Penelope's room clutching a pair of rubber gloves and a hair brush.

"Are you listening to me?" snapped Mr Masterson now.

"Yes, Sir," mumbled Royston, suddenly brought back to the present with a jerk.

"Now, I have decided after a long deliberation, to allow you to go on the school trip. You are only going, however, because it is part of our history and geography work at school and because I do not intend leaving you behind to cause even more mayhem and havoc."

"Yes, Sir."

Royston wanted to shout for joy. He could have jumped up and down on the spot and hugged the headteacher. He had imagined that the reason that Mr Masterson had sent for him that morning was to inform him that he would not be allowed to go on the school trip to the Yorkshire Moors. He drew a long happy breath, smiled widely and silently rejoiced.

"Did you hear what I just said?" asked the headteacher.

"Pardon, Sir?"

Mr Masterson put his hand to his shiny forehead and rubbed his temple as if trying to wipe away a blemish. He could feel his migraine coming on. "Let me tell you this, Royston Knapper," he continued, fixing the boy with a rattlesnake look and twisting his lips into a frightening sneer. "Mrs Gabbitas and I will be watching you like hawks, do you hear? Watching your every move. And if you so much as breathe out of place or if we so much as hear one whisper that you've been up to your old tricks, we will make you wish you had never been born. Now is that clear?"

"Yes, Sir," said Royston, giving the headteacher his fullest and most charming of smiles. "Very clear, Sir. Thank you, Sir."

The trip to Gritstone Gill in The North York Moors was a great success. Mr Masterson, Mrs Gabbitas and the children stayed in a great rambling red brick house which had been converted into a youth hostel just after the War.

It had once belonged to a wealthy landowner and he had lavished a great deal of time and money on the building. It now looked rather shabby, like a grand old lady who had seen better days. The gravel drive, which in its hey-day would have been carefully manicured by an army of gardeners, was now clotted with weeds. The once long, carefully-cropped lawns were now patched with moss and clumps of mushrooms, and the neglected borders formed one long jungle of overgrown shrubs. Inside, however, it was warm and welcoming. There were cosy bedrooms, a television room, a games area and magnificent views across the bleak moor.

The children walked for miles. They saw crashing waterfalls, explored caves, visited farms, and camped out;

and all week Royston kept out of trouble. Mr Masterson had been true to his words and watched Royston's every movement like a hawk.

It was the last night, and Mr Fawcett, the warden of the youth hostel where they were staying, had a cluster of pupils around him and was telling them about the history of the building. He was a big-nosed, big-voiced man with a round smiling face and a thatch of very thick white hair.

"This house was called Gritstone Grange, you know. Many years ago, it was a big manor house and the squire and his family lived here. There used to be beautiful furniture and velvet curtains, coloured tapestries and oil paintings everywhere; there were fancy fountains in the gardens and long green lawns with strutting peacocks. Where we are now used to be the kitchen, below stairs as they used to say, and of course they cooked all the food down here in the olden days."

"Fancy that," observed Royston. "Cooking food in a kitchen."

"Are you being cheeky?" asked Mr Fawcett, "because if you are you can always go up to bed."

"Ignore him, Mr Fawcett," said Penelope. "He's a nuisance, is Royston Knapper. He always has to make a clever comment."

"Up where you sleep," continued the warden, "were the servants' quarters. They were the bedrooms in the olden days."

"Fancy that," observed Royston. "Sleeping in the bedrooms."

"I've warned you once, young man," said Mr Fawcett, looking seriously over the top of his glasses, like a judge in

a court of law. "One more word out of you and you're up those stairs."

"Is it haunted?" asked Noleen Midgely in a frail little voice.

"Oh yes indeed," replied Mr Fawcett. "There are one or two ghosts knocking around."

"Huh!" said Royston. "What a load of rubbish!"

"Well, young man," growled Mr Fawcett. "If you lived here all year round, you'd soon change your mind."

"What sort of ghosts are they then?" asked Royston. "Vampires and zombies, big hairy monsters with great snapping jaws, ferocious ghouls and headless spectres dripping with blood?"

"No they are not," replied Mr Fawcett. "They are very nice ghosts."

"Very nice ghosts!" snorted Royston, throwing his head back. "Since when are there very nice ghosts?"

"What sort of ghosts are they, Mr Fawcett?" asked

Gillian Kershaw, giving Royston an icy stare and recalling the incident with the gas mask.

"Well, there's old Sir Digby Hainsworth," the warden told her. "He died over a hundred years ago."

"Was he murdered?" asked Micky Lincoln in a grisly voice.

"No, no, nothing so gruesome. He was fetching a bottle of port and fell down the cellar steps and broke his neck. He wanders around looking for the bottle of wine, with his head cocked on one side. He's quite harmless and rather pleasant to have around."

"I bet he's really a pain in the neck," chuckled Royston. "Get it? Pain in the neck?"

"Oh, do be quiet, Royston," sighed Penelope. "Some of us are interested in the story, even if you aren't."

"I don't think I'd like him wandering around my house," said Gillian.

"Nor mine," said Noleen nervously. "He would give me the creeps."

"You two don't need to worry," said Royston. "He wouldn't want to wander around your houses. One look at you two, and you would give *him* the creeps."

"Have there been any murders in the house, Mr Fawcett?" asked Noleen Midgely, looking decidedly ill-at-ease.

"No, not murders, but there was an accident."

"An accident?" repeated Gillian Kershaw. "What sort of accident?"

Mr Fawcett lowered his voice to a whisper. "You know that small toilet on the top landing by the large north window?"

"What happened then?" asked Royston loudly. "Did somebody flush themselves away?"

"Will you be quiet, Royston Knapper!" snapped Penelope.

Mr Fawcett continued in hushed tones: "Well, at the end of the long landing just outside that old toilet, on a wet and windy night in 1850, one of the servants – a little parlourmaid called Annie McCrudden – went to close the window that had blown open in the wind. She was only small, you see, and couldn't quite reach the shutters. She leaned out just as a gust of wind blew off the moor. She lost her balance they said, and the poor little thing fell. She tumbled out. Of course, they have safety rails up there now. We don't want children going the same way, do we?"

"How terrible," murmured Noleen. "Was she hurt?"

"Was she hurt?" repeated Royston. "What do you mean, was she hurt? You don't fall out of a window three storeys up, unless of course you happen to have a set of wings, and land on the ground saying, 'Oh dearie me, I've

grazed my knee'."

"She was found the next morning," sighed Mr Fawcett. "Dead as a doornail. It was a dreadful tragedy. They say that little Annie, who was a cheerful, bright-eyed little thing and liked by all in the household, was in love with the groom, the young man who looked after the horses, and they were going to get married. After the tragedy they say the lad was heartbroken. He never spoke for days, just mooned around in a world of his own. Then one evening he up and saddles the squire's great grey mare and gallops off into the mist, never to be seen again."

"Oooooh, how romantic," sighed Frances Partington.

"And on some nights, when the pale moon is hidden behind the dark clouds and the cold fog descends thickly like a grey cloak, some folk have been woken from their sleep by the sound of eerie clip-clopping, clip-clopping of ghostly hooves on the cobbles outside the casement window. Going to find out what the noise is, they stare from the window to see a pale figure on a grey horse, shrouded in mist, with glowing eyes. They say it is little Annie's sweetheart waiting for her."

"Aaah," sighed Noleen. "How sad."

"I don't see how they can see this ghost," observed Royston, "with the moon behind a cloud and a thick fog, unless of course they have infra-red vision."

"I didn't say they saw him clearly," retorted Mr Fawcett, becoming irritated by the frequent interruptions to his tale. "I said it was a pale figure on a grey horse, a ghostly shape."

"Ignore him, Mr Fawcett," urged Penelope, who stared up at the warden with wide eyes and her head cupped in her hands. "Go on."

"On some nights," continued Mr Fawcett in a hushed voice, "when it's cold and wet, and the wind whistles eerily through the skeletal trees, little Annie can be seen in the North corridor, just outside the small toilet, dressed in a

THE GHOST OF GRITSTONE GRANGE

white night-dress, looking dreamily through the window for her lost love."

"Aaah," sighed Frances.

"So watch out tonight, folks," interrupted Royston, "for the spectre from the lavatory, the Lady of the Loo, the Phantom of the Water Closet."

"Oh do be quiet!" snapped Penelope. "You always spoil things with your stupid comments, Royston Knapper."

"Then the little ghost of Annie wanders up and down the corridors, a-moaning and a-groaning, a-moaning and a-groaning," continued Mr Fawcett. "Calling for her lost love."

"I hope she doesn't wander into my room," said Noleen nervously.

"Nor mine," added Penelope.

"You've got nothing to fear," said Royston. "Your face is enough to put the wind up any ghost. You would give a vampire a heart attack!"

"Yes, well I'd sooner have a ghost in my room than you, Royston Knapper," replied Penelope.

"That will do, that will do," said Mr Fawcett. "You should all be turning in now. It's getting late and you've got a long journey ahead of you tomorrow."

"Mr Fawcett," said Noleen with a pale, earnest face. "I don't like the idea of little Annie coming into my room, a-moaning and a-groaning. I'm quite frightened."

"Don't worry, my dear," laughed the warden. "She's never been seen in a room, just on the corridor. Anyway, it's only a story. I don't suppose there's a whole lot of truth in it."

"Well, I think it's a load of old rubbish," announced

Royston.

"Perhaps it is," agreed the warden smiling. "And then again, perhaps it isn't."

"Have you ever seen her, Mr Fawcett?" asked Noleen nervously. The warden thought for a moment. He had indeed seen the little spectre but, bearing in mind the nervous state of the pale-faced Noleen and the time of night, he thought it better to reply that he had not.

"And don't you get any ideas, Royston Knapper," said Penelope, "about wandering into our rooms pretending to be a ghost, like you did in Switzerland, because we've got locks on our doors. And if you do disturb us, we will report you to Mr Masterson."

"I'd sooner play blind man's bluff with a charging elephant, than enter your room," replied Royston.

It was around midnight when Royston woke up. As usual he had eaten and drunk far too much at dinner and was now desperate to go to the toilet. He sat up and stared around. It looked really spooky. A flood of white light from

the cold moon lit up the room, casting eerie shadows across the walls, and a blustery wind whistled outside the window.

"Micky!" he whispered loudly to the sleeping boy in the next bed. "Micky!" He prodded him.

"Whaaaat?" moaned the boy, snuggling down further under the sheets.

"Are you asleep?"

"Yes."

"You can't be asleep, you're talking."

"I'm talking in my sleep."

"Micky!"

"Whaaaat?"

"You don't want to go to the toilet, do you?"

"No, I don't."

"Well, I do."

"Well, go then."

"It's a bit spooky. Do you fancy coming with me?"

"No, I don't. I'm in the middle of a dream where I'm scoring the winning goal for England in the Cup Final."

"Come on, Micky."

"No." The boy buried his head in the pillow and was soon snoring loudly.

Royston climbed out of bed and shivered as his toes touched the cold floor. He crept from the bedroom and down the long dark corridor. The heavy floorboards creaked under his feet and the gloomy portraits of sour-faced old men, in old-fashioned clothes, peered down at him from their frames in solemn disapproval. Their eyes seemed to follow his progress. He swallowed thickly and stared into the gloom. Pale moonlight streamed through the window at the end of the corridor and lay in blocks on the floor.

It looked like a great yawning mouth, waiting to swallow him up. A small cold dread settled into the pit of Royston's stomach.

"Oooer," he said to himself and his voice seemed to echo.

The small toilet at the end was cold and smelly, with green tiles covering the walls, and a little window through which the cold moon shone. Royston shivered. The toilet itself had a hard wooden seat and above it was a heavy black iron water tank. From this hung a long rusting chain. He pushed the door shut and felt along the cold green tiles for the light switch.

Click! Nothing happened.

"Oooer," he said again. "That's all we need."

As he sat there in the darkness, a picture of little Annie came into his mind, leaning out to pull the window shut. Then he imagined her floating through the air like a great white bird. He shivered and gripped the hard wooden seat. Suddenly, there was a creaking in the corridor outside, as if someone was opening a window. Then there was a heavy thud. Royston felt his stomach churn and his heart began to pound. His face became hot and he began to tremble. Soon he could stand it no longer and tugged at the door. It banged open against the green tiles and he hurled himself into the corridor. Then he froze. There at the end by the window, bathed in moonlight, stood a little figure dressed in white. The apparition raised its hand as if beckoning.

"Aaaaahh!" screamed Royston. "It's her! It's her! She's come for me!"

With that, he began running at great speed down the corridor, shrieking. The little figure in white stared after him in amazement.

"Now what's the matter with Royston Knapper?" said Penelope Pringle.

Harvest Time
is Here Again

The two boys crunched noisily through the crisp leaves
on their way to school.

"I love autumn," said the first, a cheeky-faced boy with
a mop of unruly ginger hair and an impish grin.

"I hate it!" complained the second, a pale, plump boy
with stiff, curly hair like a doll's. "There's piles of dead,
smelly leaves everywhere, it's damp and dark and wet, and
I always get a rotten cold. Summer holidays are gone and
Christmas is months away. I have to help my grandad dig
over his allotment, my dad tidy up the garden, and help my
mum clean the house. It's horrible and I hate it!"

"I love it," said the first boy, kicking a pile of dead, red
leaves high in the air. "I love all the bright colours and the
earthy smells."

"Oh, stop being so flipping cheerful, Royston Knapper," moaned the second boy. "I'm tired of seeing your grinning face. You look like a Cheshire cat. It's all right for you, you never bring anything to Harvest Festival, but I get loaded down with left-overs from my grandad's allotment and my mum's cupboards. I'm like a walking greengrocer's, come autumn. I hate it!"

"Oh, do stop moaning will you, Fozzy," said his friend, kicking up another huge pile of leaves, "you'll have me crying in a minute."

"Well, I hate autumn, and I really, really hate having to fetch to school these tins of smelly spaghetti, boxes of apples and bags of vegetables for Harvest Festival."

"I never bother bringing anything," said Royston. "There's never anything to bring. There's never any apples left on our tree. Come to think of it, there's never any apples left on the neighbours' trees either. And our pantry's permanently empty. My mum says I'm like a human dustbin. She just gives me some money for the school to buy stuff. It's much easier."

"I wish my mum would," sighed Fozzy, struggling under his heavy load. "But she uses it as an excuse to clear the pantry of all the old tins and food we never eat. Another thing I hate about all this Harvest Festival carry-on, is having to take baskets of food to all the pensioners. I always end up with a really bad-tempered old man who has a vicious Rottweiler the size of a horse, or a killer cat, or a bad-tempered parrot that plops all over you. Last year, I had old Mr Osbaldiston from Jubilee Villas. He never stopped complaining."

The boy put on a wheedling sort of voice. " 'Kids

these days don't know they're born; they want a good
hiding; never did me any harm; they have it too soft; they
have no consideration for others; when you get old nobody
wants you'. Well, I certainly wouldn't want Mr Osbaldiston
in our house. Moan, moan, moan."

"Sounds to me as if you two have a lot in common,"
observed Royston.

Fozzy ignored the interruption. "It was horrible –
really, really horrible last year. He moaned and groaned
about how the oranges were over-ripe and would give him
wind; how he only liked Granny Smith apples - the ones in
the basket were too small and sour; how he never ate
anything out of a tin because you could get lead poisoning;
and how the Bourbon biscuits were stale! 'And you've spelt
my name wrong,' he said, as I was trying to get my foot out
of his dog's mouth. I'm not going back there again. I had
nightmares for a week afterwards."

"I still see my pensioner," said Royston cheerfully. "I wave to him every morning on the way to school. He wears jeans and plays pop music all day, hardly ever washes and chews this black tobacco all the time, and sometimes he curses and swears. I'm going to be like Mr Gomersall when I get old."

"As far as I can remember," said Fozzy, still struggling with his harvest burden, "you were in trouble, as usual, after last year's Harvest Festival. You set off for that old man's house with a box full of stuff - biscuits, fruit, sweets, cheese - and when you got there, all that was left was a jar of meat paste and a shrivelled turnip."

"Well, I got a bit peckish on the way," admitted Royston. "Anyway, Mr Gomersall didn't mind. He said I was a good lad for coming and gave me twenty pence."

"I'll tell you this, Royston Knapper: if you fell into a mountain of smelly manure, you'd come out smelling of roses."

As they turned into the road leading to Bogglesview School, the two boys nearly collided with a tall, thin man with stringy hair and a sharp beak of a nose. He was wearing a long, grey raincoat and carrying a large black briefcase.

"Oh, excuse me, boys," said the man brightly. "I wonder if you could help me?"

"No," said Royston and walked round him.

"I beg your pardon?" said the man, startled by the bluntness of the reply.

"I said no, we can't help you."

"But how do you know that you can't help me, if you don't know what it is I want to know?"

"I don't want to know what you want me to know, so on your bike!"

"You're a very cheeky boy," said the man. "A very, very cheeky boy, indeed."

"Go away," said Royston. "We've been told not to talk to strange, suspicious-looking men in dirty raincoats."

"Look here!" said the man, his face colouring with embarrassment. "I am not strange and I do not wear a dirty raincoat. Now, can you please tell me where Cornfield School is?"

"I can, but I'm not going to."

"Now, look here …" began the man.

"If you don't go away," said Royston calmly, "I'll shout for the police and kick you on the shins. I must warn you that I've got a very loud voice and I take karate lessons. My pal here also does kick-boxing."

"What is your name?" asked the man, staring at Royston coldly, like a serpent.

"Mary Poppins," replied Royston. "And this is my friend, Humpty Dumpty."

"Very well," said the man angrily. "I'll find the school myself!" and he strode away in the opposite direction.

"What was all that about?" asked Royston's companion.

"Don't you ever listen, Fozzy? Don't you remember when P.C. Hardcastle talked to the whole school about not accepting lifts from strangers, or talking to suspicious-looking men outside school? He probably wanted to kidnap me, drag me off in his car and then ask for a ransom."

"Anybody who wants to kidnap you, Royston," replied Fozzy, smiling for the first time that day, "wants his head examining. After a couple of days he'd pay your parents to have you back!"

"P.C. Hardcastle said, 'Never talk to strangers outside school,' that's what he said."

"Since when have you ever listened to anything grown-ups say?" asked Fozzy. "And another thing, I don't do kick-boxing."

The two boys arrived at school just as the whistle blew. They walked slowly across the playground, which was littered with bits of conker and string, squelchy leaves and long, grey puddles.

"I really hate autumn," said Fozzy. "It's really, really horrible."

Inside the school it was bright and warm and noisy, and smelt of disinfectant and floor polish and fruit. Children were pushing and arguing, chattering and laughing, taking off coats and sitting on benches, playing conkers and telling jokes.

Through the crowd, Royston Knapper caught sight of his dreaded enemy, Penelope Pringle. He had disliked Penelope Pringle since the Infants, when she had told Mrs Gregory, the headteacher, that he had done a wee in the sand-pit. He had accidentally-on-purpose poured his milk down the front of her pinafore dress and was made to stand in the corner facing the wall for half an hour.

"Oi, Pringly!" he shouted above the heads of the other children. "It's nearly Hallowe'en - have you ordered your pointed hat and broomstick yet?"

"I thought you were hibernating, Royston Knapper," Penelope shouted back, "along with the other rodents."

For the first part of the morning, Royston's class was kept busy composing poems on autumn.

"Now, I want some really good efforts," said Mrs Gabbitas. "Lots of lovely, interesting words, vivid adjectives, imaginative phrases and colourful images and plenty of description and lively rhythms."

"Miss, do we have to write a poem?" groaned Fozzy. "I hate poems and I hate autumn. Can I write a science fiction story about aliens from outer space?"

"Yes, we do have to write a poem, Jamie Foster," replied Mrs Gabbitas, "and no, you cannot write a story about aliens from outer space. Every piece of writing I seem to get from you is about man-eating aliens from Mars, or blood-sucking monsters that take over the planet. There are other things in the world to write about."

Fozzy slumped back on his chair. "AAAggghhh, Miss!"

"And don't make that silly noise, Jamie. You sound as if you're choking on a bone. I don't want to see that dreadful face either. One day the wind will change and your face will stay like that." Mrs Gabbitas's offhand tone signalled an end to the discussion.

"Miss, can we do a rap poem?" asked Royston Knapper brightly.

"No, you cannot do a rap poem," replied Mrs Gabbitas sharply.

"Miss, there's lots of lively rhythms in a rap poem." Royston began clicking his fingers and moving his body to the rhythm. "We got beans, we got greens, we got juicy tangerines, we got dates, we got grapes, we got ..."

"You are not writing a rap poem, Royston Knapper," interrupted the teacher, with growing impatience, "and that is that. I want some nice, descriptive, peaceful poems. The best ones will be read out at tomorrow's Harvest Festival Service at St Walburga's and I'm not having you jumping up and down in the church like some kangaroo with fleas, performing a rap poem. I am sure Mr Masterson does not want a repetition of last year's fiasco, which, from what I hear, had you at the centre."

"Me, Miss?" exclaimed Royston, putting on his most innocent expression.

Penelope Pringle was the first pupil to take her poem out to the teacher and Mrs Gabbitas looked particularly pleased as she read the first effort.

"Now, Penelope's poem," she said enthusiastically to the class, "captures perfectly the mood of autumn, and it will set the tone of the Harvest Festival Service very nicely. Read it out, will you dear?"

Penelope coughed theatrically and began reading her poem in a pleased-as-punch, sing-song sort of voice:

> "Apples are red upon the tree,
> Big fat pears for all to see.
> Fields of oats and barns of grain,
> Autumn time is here again.

Leaves a-fluttering to the ground,
Landing lightly, not a sound.
Gusty winds and heavy rain,
Autumn time is here again."

There followed another five verses, all delivered in identical sing-song tones, and ending with the same line, which pupils began to join in with as the poem progressed.

All through the reading, Royston scowled and sniffed and coughed and fidgeted. Then, he picked up his pencil and twirled it thoughtfully between his thumb and forefinger, before writing furiously. He slid a scrap of paper to Timothy Joseph who, after reading it, winced and held his breath to keep from giggling. But he could not contain himself for long and suddenly burst into gales of laughter:

"See her swing from tree to tree,
Just like Tarzan's chimpanzee,
It's the girl without a brain.
Penelope Pringle is her name.

See her flying through the sky,
On her broomstick way up high,
Smelling like a great big drain.
Penelope Pringle is her name."

"Timothy Joseph!" shouted Mrs Gabbitas angrily.

"Yes, Miss," replied Tim, trying to suppress his laughter by stuffing his handkerchief in his mouth.

"What seems to be amusing you?" She eyed him acidly.

"Nothing, Miss," mumbled Tim.

"Well something clearly occasioned that disgraceful and very silly behaviour!"

"Miss, I was just thinking about my poem, Miss," said Tim feebly.

"Well, let us all share in your obvious amusement, Timothy." There was a note of sharp command in her voice. "I'm sure we will all be entertained by your amazing effort." She paused and fixed Tim with her eyes. "Well, Timothy, off you go."

Tim, blushing and squirming, with all eyes trained in his direction, began his reading in a stumbling voice:

"Bananas are yeller,
Apples are red,
When autumn comes,
I stop in bed."

"Is that it?" asked Mrs Gabbitas, raising an eyebrow.
"Yes, Miss," replied Tim.
"Hardly William Wordsworth, are you, Timothy?
I think we will give that poem a miss tomorrow. Perhaps your partner in crime has displayed a little more thought and effort with his poem. Off you go, Royston."

Royston stood up, took a deep breath, coughed lightly and began:

"When autumn comes we all go bonkers,
Bashing other people's conkers."

"Well, that will certainly not be read out in church, either," announced Mrs Gabbitas. "Right you two, come down to the front and sit where I can see you. You can join them, Jamie Foster, since you are still pulling that grumpy face. I want a nice, colourful poem before break from each of you."

When Mrs Gabbitas was busy sorting out the autumn offerings, Royston caught Penelope's eye and did a pretty fair impression of 'The Creature from the Black Lagoon'. Penelope gave him a contemptuous look and added a further two verses to her poem.

Just before morning break, Mr Masterson, the headteacher, appeared with a little tubby man, bald and beaming, with a halo of white hair.

"I'm sorry to interrupt, Mrs Gabbitas, but the vicar and I would like a couple of words with your class about tomorrow."

Mr Masterson turned to face the children. "Put your pens and pencils down for one moment please, and look this way. The Reverend Windthrush and I just want to say a few things about Friday's service. Before I hand you over to the vicar, I want to remind you all that we will be in church and not Wembley Stadium. Last year's silly behaviour, when several oranges were kicked about the church, will not be repeated. Is that clear, Royston Knapper?"

"Sir, it wasn't me," protested the boy.

"It never is, Royston," replied the headteacher. "It never is. Now this year we will be having a very important person joining us."

"The Queen, Sir?" asked Noleen Midgely in an ecstatic voice.

"No, Noleen, not the Queen, but one of her very own school inspectors, Mr Craddock. He's a very important school inspector and I don't need to remind you all about behaving yourselves. Mr Craddock is visiting schools in the area this week and will be with us tomorrow. I want him to leave for London with a very good impression of Bogglesview School. I hope I make myself perfectly plain!" Mr Masterson's eyes were trained on Royston Knapper, like a hungry cat watching a goldfish in a tank.

"Yes, Sir," chorused the class.

"Good! Now I'm going to ask the Reverend Windthrush to say a few words about Friday's arrangements. Over to you, vicar."

Reverend Windthrush rubbed his fat little hands and beamed. "Thank you, thank you Mr Masterson. Good morning children. I must say it is very nice to come into your bright, cheerful school this morning. Isn't autumn a lovely time of the year?" Fozzy scowled.

"And what a delightful selection of harvest produce you have brought in. How very kind. The elderly people in the parish will be so grateful." Fozzy, recalling the whingeing tones and miserable expression of Mr Osbaldiston, screwed up his face even more and muttered under his breath.

"When I saw those fat, juicy, red apples on the table over there, I was very tempted to pick one up and have a great big bite, like a very famous person in the Garden of Eden thousands of years ago. I wonder if anybody knows about whom I am talking?"

A forest of hands went up. Royston, who was busy showing Tim another verse of his poem about Penelope Pringle, had not heard a word. The vicar continued smiling and in a soft and friendly voice, directed his question at Fozzy.

"Do you know who took the first apple off the tree, young man?"

Fozzy shot up in his chair, startled. "Pardon?" He had not been listening either, but thinking of another possible trip to the home of the disagreeable pensioner.

"Who took the apple from the tree?" repeated Reverend Windthrush, smiling broadly.

"Wasn't me, vicar, honest," said Fozzy. "I don't like apples."

"And it wasn't me either," said Royston. "So I don't know why everybody's looking in my direction."

Mr Masterson sighed. "This is what I have to contend with, Reverend Windthrush. That is the boy who I have an idea made the animal noises last year, clucking his way through the service."

"Dear me," said the vicar, "I thought somebody had brought a hen into church. What with that and the oranges it turned out to be quite a lively service. However, let's get on. Now, tomorrow children, after the opening hymn 'All Things Bright and Beautiful', I shall give a short introduction and read a passage from the Bible. It comes from a very famous prophet of the Old Testament, called Isaiah, and begins:

> 'This year and next year you will have only wild grain to eat, but the following year you will be able to sow your corn and harvest it, and plant vine and grapes.'

Now, later in the passage, Isaiah compares the people to sheep."

"And we don't want any sheep noises, Royston Knapper!" Mr Masterson added.

The vicar smiled sheepishly. "Why do you think the prophet compared people to sheep?"

Timothy Joseph's hand shot up. "Was it because they had long hair and wore sheepskin jackets?"

"No, not really," said the vicar, realising that his attempt to extract information from the class was failing dismally.

"They acted like sheep by copying each other, instead of thinking for themselves," said Penelope confidently.

"Very good," chortled the vicar. "That is right. Now, after my reading there will be some autumn poems read by you, the pupils of the school."

"And we have some very nice ones too, Reverend Windthrush," announced Mrs Gabbitas.

"Excellent," said the vicar. "Then we will have another hymn – 'We Plough the Fields and Scatter, the Good Seed on the Land' - during which, some of the harvest produce will be brought down to the front of the church, carefully, by the children and placed before the altar. I shall finish with a short prayer."

"And I want it all to go like clockwork," said Mr Masterson, slowly and deliberately. "Mrs Gabbitas and I will be keeping our eagle eyes on certain persons, so be warned. I want the school inspector, Mr Craddock, to return to London with a lasting impression of the children of Bogglesview School."

On Friday afternoon after the service, Mr Craddock did indeed return to London with a lasting impression of Bogglesview School. However, it was not the favourable one that Mr Masterson had hoped for.

Unfortunately, the school inspector was unable to be at the church for the start of the service. Mr Masterson was so keen on showing the inspector all the work the pupils had produced, that by the time they arrived at St. Walburga's, the Harvest Festival was well under way. It was a pity Mr Craddock missed the opening part of the service, for that was the only part that went according to plan.

The service opened well enough. All the children, particularly Royston, sang loudly and lustily, if a little off-key. This was followed by a short talk by the vicar on 'being a good neighbour', particularly to the old people in the neighbourhood. Fozzy stared up at the vicar's fleshy,

shining face and pulled a gruesome expression when he
heard this, thinking all the while about Mr Osbaldiston and
his moaning and groaning, complaining and grumbling. It
was during the vicar's introductory remarks that things took
a turn for the worse.

On the way to St Walburga's, Simon Morgan had been
tempted by the fat, juicy gooseberries in his harvest basket.
One after the other he popped the gooseberries, which
weren't quite ripe, into his mouth, until they had all gone.
As Simon sat listening to the vicar, the fermenting fruit
began to churn and react in his stomach. Simon's face
turned to the colour of dripping and then to the colour of the
gooseberries themselves – a bright shade of green. Then he
was sick. Actually, he was very sick. He was sick all over
his clothes and the pew, and the hymn book, and the floor,
and finally all over Gillian Kershaw who was sitting in front.

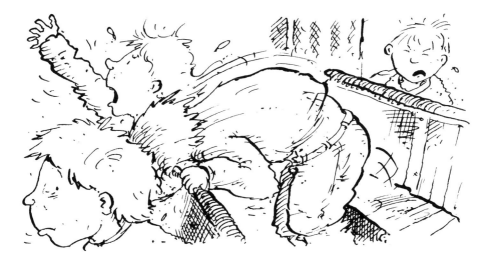

Poor Simon dashed to the nearest exit. Gillian promptly had hysterics and all the pupils in the vicinity let out loud and various 'Uuuurgggh' and 'Eeerrhhhh' noises.

The vicar, fearing a resurgence of the animal noises which had disrupted his service the previous year, paused in his reading and peered helplessly from the pulpit, a woeful expression appearing on his face. The distraught Gillian was helped out of the church by a sympathetic Mrs Gabbitas, whose loud voice echoed around the stone pillars: "There's nothing at all to cry about, Gillian. Simon didn't do it on purpose. Vomiting is quite a natural human function – we all do it."

The sickly smell soon wafted round the church, and when Penelope got up to read her poem on autumn, her nose was screwed up and her lips clamped tightly together. Penelope was just starting, when Mr Masterson and the school inspector entered the church and sat unobtrusively at the back. Mr Masterson was just about to comment on the fresh, fruity smell of autumn, but as he sniffed the air in the church he thought better of it.

Penelope launched into her epic poem. Each of the verses ended with the line: 'Autumn time is here again'. After five verses, the pupils began to get restless, fidgeting and scratching and sniffing like gerbils. Even the vicar could be seen glancing at his watch. But Penelope soldiered on:

> "Rats and mice and shrews and voles,
> Scurry to their little holes,
> Hiding from the wind and rain.
> Autumn time is here again.

Tractors with their heavy loads,
Trundle lazily down the roads,
Passing lorry, car and train.
Autumn time is here again."

"As if we didn't know," remarked Royston to Timothy
Joseph in a loud whisper. Hearing this, Penelope became
flustered and dropped her papers, which fluttered around the
church. Royston retrieved them and handed them back to
Penelope who snatched them from him, unaware that he had
slid an extra sheet of paper into her batch. Royston had
included a little poem of his own. Penelope read the verse
composed by Royston before she realised what she had said:

"Doctors round the world agree,
She's as thick as any tree.
Daft as a brush and quite insane,
And Penelope Pringle is her name."

When Mrs Gabbitas had restored order, the service continued and the organ struck up with : 'We Plough the Fields and Scatter, the Good Seed on the Land.' Pupils began filing down to the front, bringing with them the various baskets and boxes. Fozzy was loaded down with harvest fare. It was piled up in front of him so high, that he didn't see the remains of Simon Morgan's unfortunate accident on the stone floor. Fozzy slipped just as the pupils got to the word 'scatter'. And that's exactly what Fozzy did.

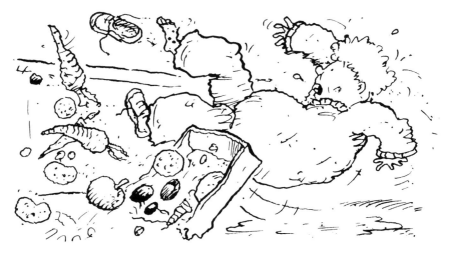

He scattered the whole armful in every direction. Apples and oranges, turnips and parsnips, potatoes and plums rolled everywhere, like billiard balls on a snooker table.

Royston could not contain his laughter any longer. He heaved and shuddered, spluttered and wheezed, until a heavy hand clutched at his shoulder.

"Down to the back of the church, you!" It was a furious, red-faced Mr Masterson. "You can sit with me and Mr Craddock, where I can keep my eye on you!"

When Royston saw the school inspector sitting on the back row, his heart missed a beat. He recognised the stringy hair and a sharp beak of a nose. It was the man who had stopped him outside school to ask directions to Cornfield School, the tall man in the raincoat.

"Sit there, you silly boy!" snapped the headteacher angrily, with a fierce light in his eye. "Next to Mr Craddock!" Mr Masterson turned to the inspector. "This lad, Mr Craddock, is the worst-behaved pupil it has ever been my misfortune to teach."

"We have met," said Mr Craddock casually, giving Royston a sickly smile. "Hello, Mary. It is Mary Poppins, isn't it?"

As Royston sat there quaking, sandwiched between the smug-faced inspector and a furious-faced Mr Masterson, he wished he was indeed Mary Poppins with a magic umbrella that would whisk him away. Then he heard the vicar's voice floating up from the front of the church, solemnly declaring: "Here endeth the first lesson."

The Report

Mr Knapper waved the long brown envelope in front of Royston's face. "And what's this?" he demanded.

Royston didn't answer, but looked up sheepishly. He knew very well what it was.

"I'll tell you what it is," continued his father, by now almost purple with anger. "I'll tell you what it is! It's your school report, that's what it is!"

Royston felt like replying, 'If you know what it is, then why are you asking me?' but he had the sense to keep very quiet and put on the very sad and sorry expression he kept for these times. He knew what his father was like when he got in one of his tempers. He was like a bear with a sore tooth.

Mrs Knapper, who was sitting knitting, also remained silent. She also knew it was unwise to interrupt her husband when he was in full flow.

"And do you know where your mother found your report?" continued Royston's father.

Royston knew exactly where his mum had found the report. It was screwed up at the bottom of his school bag, where he had stuffed it last Friday.

"No," he replied, almost in a whisper.

"I'll tell you where it was. It was found screwed up at the bottom of your school bag, where it's been since last Friday."

Mrs Knapper stopped knitting, looked up, and made a sort of clucking noise. She gave her son a pitying look.

Royston had been reading a book at school called 'A Tale of Two Cities' by Charles Dickens, in which there was a character called Madame Defage, who sat by the guillotine, knitting away. She had a stony expression on her face and never said anything. She never moved, she just watched the proceedings with mute attention, knitting and

49

nodding as the massive blade descended and chopped off people's heads. Royston thought how like Madame Defage his mother looked at that moment and how much he felt like someone facing execution.

"Are you listening to what I'm saying?" continued his father, still shouting and waving the report.

"Yes, Dad."

"And the only reason your mother found out that there was a school report in the first place is that she met Mrs Pringle in the supermarket, and she told her how her Penelope had got all these glowing comments from the teacher."

Typical, thought Royston, that Penelope Pringle should be the cause of all his troubles, yet again. "It just sort of slipped my mind. I clean forgot," Royston told his father.

"I would have thought that a report like this would be very difficult to forget. It's the worst report that I have ever seen in my whole life."

Royston wondered how many school reports his dad had ever seen in his whole life. It could only be a handful. After all, it wasn't as if his dad was a teacher or anything like that. I mean, he thought to himself, his father couldn't come across many school reports driving a number 89 bus or talking with the other drivers at the bus depot where he worked. His father was running his finger down the paper, shaking his head and making grunting noises like a bad-tempered hippopotamus.

"Look at this comment for English!" He stabbed the paper with his finger. "'Now that I have finally deciphered Royston's untidy scrawl, I have discovered that his spelling is appalling!' And this one for Maths: 'If Royston devoted as

much of his time and energy to his Maths as he does to
acting the fool, he would be another Einstein!' And the
comment for Geography is no better: 'Royston clearly has
the ability but he can be a very outspoken and noisy boy,
and he has made little progress this term!' And listen to this
one for Art: 'Royston manages to get more paint on himself
and other pupils than he does on the paper!' Then there's
games: 'The point of football is to kick the ball, not the
other players, something which seems to have escaped
Royston's notice!' I'm just lost for words."

His dad was certainly not lost for words, thought
Royston to himself, as he awaited another outburst. But his
father continued to stare at the report, shaking his head and
pulling faces.

The only noise to break the silence was the click,
clack, click, clack, click, clack of Mrs Knapper's knitting
needles. His mother was knitting a romper suit for Mrs
Griffith's daughter next door who was expecting a baby in

51

the spring. The suit was a mixture of electric blue and
bright salmon pink. It looked revolting and big enough to fit
a baby elephant. Royston's mum thought that knitting
something in blue and pink was a very sensible idea. It
wouldn't matter then whether the new arrival was a boy or a
girl.

"Well, I'm waiting." His father had finished shouting,
had placed the report on the table and was now standing
with folded arms and a stony expression like a great Eastern
statue. "What have you got to say for yourself?"

"It's not very good," replied Royston quietly.

"Huh! Not very good? Not very good?" Mr Knapper
exploded again. "It's atrocious, that's what it is. Appalling,
shocking, disgraceful! If I'd have brought a report home like
this when I was your age, my father would have tanned my
hide."

Royston couldn't imagine his grandfather beating
anyone. He was such a happy, good-natured old man.

"Mind you," continued Mr Knapper. "I blame the
teachers for a lot of this. They're too soft with children
today. They don't have the discipline. I see it on the buses.
Children screaming and shouting, and running up and down
the stairs. And smoking! They have it far too easy at school.
Kids get away with murder these days. When I was at
school, a good whack of the slipper or six of the best across
the backside sorted everybody out. It never did me any
harm, I can tell you."

Mrs Knapper placed her knitting on the table next to
the report. "They were very strict with us at the girls'
school, too," she added. "I remember a really unpleasant
little French teacher – only about five feet tall she was –

52

called Mademoiselle Farfadet. My goodness, she could inflict all variety of tortures with her metre rule. She had this big bowl of artificial fruit on her desk, which she used for drawing classes. Once, she got so angry with Evelyn Brown – she was a very talkative girl, with red hair, who sat in the corner of the classroom – that Mademoiselle Farfadet picked up a plastic banana and hurled it at poor Evelyn. It hit her smack on the top of her head, then it rebounded like some huge yellow boomerang and Mademoiselle Farfadet caught it. I shall never forget the look of astonishment on her face. Then, of course, we all started to laugh. Until she brought out the metre rule."

"Doris," said Royston's dad, "we are not reminiscing about our schooldays. We are trying to impress upon Royston here how angry and disappointed we are with his dreadful report."

"Well, it's not very good," observed Mrs Knapper.

"I know it's not very good, Doris." Mr Knapper

punctuated each word. "I have just been saying that for the last ten minutes." He turned his attention back to Royston and Mrs Knapper resumed her knitting.

"Trouble seems to surround you," Royston's dad continued. "You're always up to something, always upsetting people, getting into mischief, not doing as you are told." His dad was sounding more and more like Mr Masterson, thought Royston. "Well, until you decide to behave yourself, I'm stopping your pocket money."

"Aaw, Dad!" cried Royston, jumping up as if someone had poked him with a cattle prod.

"And your skateboard stays in the shed!"

"Aaw, Dad!"

"And you can forget about going out with your friends on Saturday as well."

"Aaw, Dad!"

"Don't 'Aaw, Dad' me. You've brought it on yourself. Until I see a big improvement in your behaviour, young man, there will be no pocket money, your skateboard stays locked in the garage and you stay at home. And don't go asking your grandad for any money when you see him this afternoon."

Royston visited his grandad most Saturday afternoons. Old Mr Knapper lived in a small, shiny, red-brick terraced house with a greasy, grey-slate roof, a cluttered backyard and an outside toilet. Royston's mum said that inside the house was like a junk shop and needed a good clear out, but Royston's grandad would have none of that. He had lived in the house all his life and Royston's dad had been born and brought up in it. Old Mr Knapper had, over the years, accumulated a mass of varied and interesting but, for the most part, quite useless objects. 'You never know when they might come in handy,' he told Royston's mother, when she asked why he kept some unusable object or other.

Royston liked the cellar. It was cold and damp with a musty smell, and was full of jars and bottles, tins and boxes, bike frames, old tools, and broken furniture. But he liked the attic better. It was different. It was an Aladdin's Cave, dark, dusty and full of mystery. There were old leather-bound books, broken cameras and chipped ornaments, faded carpets and cracked mirrors, chipped vases and broken clocks, bundles of worn clothes and albums full of old photographs and postcards. It was in the attic that Royston had found the World War II gas mask which had got him into all that trouble.

On some Saturdays, Royston and his grandad went up into the attic. They'd sit on two old tea chests and Royston would listen to the old man as he recounted one of the exciting adventures of his youth. In every story his grandad featured as the hero. He'd shot down the infamous 'Red Baron' in a furious 'dog fight' when his aircraft was

belching out flames and smoke; he'd rescued an Eastern prince from certain death at the hands of a hoard of bloodthirsty Dervishes (that was when his grandad had been in the Foreign Legion); he'd been the last passenger to jump off the Titanic as the huge liner sank beneath the icy waters; codenamed Escargot, he had been the British spy who foiled the kidnap attempt on the Prime Minister, by the evil Russian agent, Ivan Rottenstintsky. Royston knew that every one of the stories was made up, but he loved listening to them. His grandad reckoned that his grandson had inherited his wild and wonderful imagination.

That Saturday afternoon, Royston was helping old Mr Knapper look for some rolls of wallpaper in the attic, where they had been stored several years before.

"What's the matter with you today?" asked his grandad. "You've got a face like a wet Wednesday."

"Dad went barmy when he saw my school report. Said it was the worst one he'd ever seen. And he's stopped my pocket money. I can't even use my skateboard and I've got to stop in on Saturdays until I behave myself."

"Oh dear," sighed the old man. "That's not so good, is it? You ought to do your schoolwork, you know, Royston. You'll not get a very good job if you don't get your exams. Mind you, I was just the same when I was at school. Always in scrapes I was, always ending up in the headmaster's room for a whacking. I think being a bit lively and mischievous runs in the Knapper family. I remember your Uncle Michael was always getting into trouble. Did I ever tell you about the time he borrowed your grandma's best leather gloves to play goalie?"

"No, Grandad," said Royston sadly.

"She looked high and low for those gloves and then, one day, as she was passing the school, she saw Michael in the playground wearing them. He didn't half get a telling off."

"That's what I've just got from my dad," the boy told his grandad.

The old man put his arm around his grandson's shoulder. "You don't want to get so upset, Royston. It's not the end of the world. You're a good lad at heart, just a bit on the mischievous side. But you do need to work hard at school, you know. I never did, and I wish I had now."

"I bet Dad worked really hard at school and never got into trouble." The old man remained silent. "Did he, Grandad?"

"Did he what?"

"Work really hard at school and never get into trouble?"

"Is that what he's told you?"

"Well, he's always telling me how good he was."

"Aye, well, he's a Knapper all right. He's got that wild and wonderful imagination that I was telling you about, has your dad. It runs in the family."

"What do you mean, Grandad?"

"Never you mind, young Royston. Is that the wallpaper we were looking for, at the back of you? Under that old carpet?"

Royston rummaged under the carpet. He didn't find the wallpaper but what he did find was much more interesting. It was a small, sandalwood box, full of old photographs and papers.

"What's this, Grandad?" asked Royston.

"Pass it over," said the old man. He put on his spectacles. "Oh yes, I wondered where this box had got to. It's got all your dad's school photos in and his swimming medals, and look at this, it's his old school cap badge." He passed the box over to Royston, who examined the photographs, smiling.

"Is this my dad on the end? Crikey, he looks a bit podgy, Grandad, doesn't he?"

"Aye, he was on the generous side when he was a lad."

"What's this?" asked Royston, opening a small piece of faded paper. "Look, it's my dad's school report."

"Well I never," chuckled the old man, a twinkle in his eye. "I think you'd better take the box and give it to your dad. He'll enjoy looking through those photos and things, and remembering what a good boy he was at school. Now see if you can find that wallpaper, will you? I know it's up here somewhere."

When Royston arrived home he found his dad reading the paper in the front room.

"I hope you didn't ask your grandad for any money," were his dad's first words.

"I didn't," replied Royston.

"Or bring any of his old rubbish home with you. You've got enough stuff in your bedroom to start a junk shop."

"He gave me this." Royston held out the box.

"What is it?"

"It's a box full of photos and things. They were yours when you were at school."

"Let's have a look," said Royston's dad, folding up the newspaper and reaching out for the box.

"Oh I say, look at this," he chuckled. "I remember when this photo was taken. Dear oh dear! Just look at the state of me! We used to have our hair short in those days. Short back and sides. And look at those trousers! 'Course, we were in shorts until we were twelve."

Mr Knapper was still chuckling to himself when he opened his old school report. Suddenly, his expression changed and his face took on a red tinge. "Oh, er...I didn't know these were in here...my old school reports. Have you...er...had a look at these, Royston?"

"Just a quick glance," replied Royston, putting on his innocent expression. "Of course, they're full of long words that I don't understand, words like 'disruptive' and 'hyperactive', and 'prone to mischief', things like that."

"Yes, well, they used fancy words in those days."

"What do they mean, Dad?"

"Oh, they have lots of meanings...I...er...wouldn't worry your head about them...it was a long time ago."

"Mum will know what they mean when she comes in."

"Your mother doesn't want to be bothered with that sort of thing. She's got enough on her plate at the moment."

"I know, Dad, but Mrs Gabbitas, our teacher, says we should always ask if we don't understand…"

"Why don't you take your skateboard and fetch me a paper from the corner shop?"

"But you've already got one and anyway you said I'm not allowed to take my skateboard out until I behave…"

"I know what I said, but I've changed my mind. And don't say anything to your mum about those school reports." He folded them into a square and pushed them into his pocket.

"Have you changed your mind about my pocket money as well, Dad?"

There was a cheeky expression on Royston's face.

"There is a word you ought to know the meaning of, and that's 'incorrigible'. How much do I owe you?"

"Five pounds," replied Royston. "And, Dad, shall I put your old school reports at the bottom of my school bag for safe keeping?"

Buster

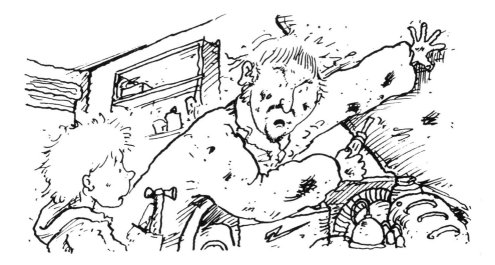

"No!" snapped Royston's father from under the bonnet of the car. He was busy in the garage, tinkering about with the engine. "And don't ask again."

"Aww, Dad," groaned Royston. "It's only for a week. Two at the most."

"Royston," said his father, emerging from under the bonnet and wiping his hands on a great oily rag, "I said no, and let that be the end of it."

"But what is Mr Gomersall going to do?" Royston asked plaintively.

"I don't know what Mr Gomersall is going to do, and frankly I don't care. That's his business. It has nothing to do with us."

"But I said we'd have it," Royston told his father, sadly.

"Well we can't! You had no business telling him that. You can go round right now and tell Mr Gomersall that we are very sorry but we can't."

"But, Dad …." began Royston.

"Royston, I shall say this for the very last time. We are not, I repeat not, looking after Mr Gomersall's dog. I don't like dogs and dogs don't like me, and we are not having another pet in this house. I haven't forgotten all the trouble we had when you brought the school hamster home for the holidays. I had to have the floorboards up, the washer out, the cupboards off, the shelves down, looking for that wretched rodent after you let it escape from its cage – and then we found it in your bed!"

"But he's going into hospital." Royston put on his pleading expression.

"Yes, you told me. Well, I'm very sorry to hear that and I hope Mr Gomersall gets better soon, but we are not having his dog. Let him put it in a kennel."

"It would pine away. It's such a soft, affectionate, sensitive, gentle, loveable, little pooch that it would …"

"Royston!" roared Mr Knapper, angrily throwing down the oily rag and grasping his son by the shoulders. "We are not having that dog!"

Royston had taken the harvest basket of fruit, vegetables and biscuits to Mr Gomersall, as he had done the previous year. The old man had been delighted to see him because he received few visitors, and Royston had spent a good hour looking at old photographs and talking about all sorts of things. The old man had told Royston that he had to go into hospital for a week, or maybe two, to have an operation on his 'gammy leg'. He had said how worried he was about his dog who would miss him so much. Who would look after him while he was away?

Mr Gomersall's dog, Buster, was far from the soft, affectionate, sensitive, gentle, loveable little pooch Royston had described to his father. In fact, it was the very opposite. Buster was a bulldog – a fat, barrel-bodied, bow-legged, repellent beast with teeth as sharp as tank traps and the grey button eyes of a killer shark. When Royston had first visited Mr Gomersall, the vicious looking monster had cornered him, made a low throaty rumbling noise like a distant train, showed his impressive set of teeth and eyed him hungrily as he might a juicy bone.

"Give over, Buster, stop showing off!" Mr Gomersall had told the creature. "He won't hurt you Royston. Just ignore him… but don't move for a minute though. He tends to bite things that move. Wait until something else catches his attention and then walk slowly over here, casual-like, and don't look afraid. He can sense fear, can Buster. I tell you one thing Royston, I don't need locks on my doors. If a

burglar was foolhardy enough to break into this house, he'd
have a nasty shock in store and no mistake. Of course,
Buster would let him in." The old man paused for a moment.
"But he'd not let him out." Mr Gomersall chuckled and
rubbed his chin. "You see, a bulldog's teeth lock. They
hang on like billy-o. They clamp like a man trap. Once he
bites you, there's no way of prising Buster's jaws apart."

Royston had found it very difficult to ignore the dog as
Mr Gomersall had suggested, particularly after the little
description of its amazing capabilities, and also because
Buster had followed him around, sniffing and growling and
rumbling and eyeing him. Since then, Royston had called in
a few times to see Mr Gomersall and on each visit the dog
seemed to have become more accustomed to him. It
growled and rumbled rather less, but Royston still felt it
could not be trusted and stood stock still when the creature
approached. Buster could not, however, be remotely
described as friendly, and he was certainly not a soft,
affectionate, sensitive, gentle, loveable, little pooch!

Mr Gomersall had explained that his worry about his
impending operation was nothing compared to the concern
he felt for Buster's welfare. The neighbours wouldn't look
after the dog. They were terrified of the creature. As was
the postman, who delivered the letters next door; the
milkman, who left the milk at the gate; the paperboy, who
threw the paper over the hedge, and the meals-on-wheels
lady who was last seen heading at high speed down the
garden path - covered in gravy and custard. Mr Gomersall
had learnt later that the poor woman had given up the meals-
on-wheels job to take on a less stressful position as a traffic
warden! People only tended to call at the house once,

Mr Gomersall had explained to Royston. The unsuspecting man collecting for the RSPCA had suffered the same fate as the meals-on-wheels lady, and he too had sprinted for the street pursued by Buster, little stick-on badges fluttering like confetti in the wind and the collecting tin bouncing in the gutter. Buster had got him at the gate. The poor man had never made a return visit, and his experience with Buster had quite changed his view of poor defenceless animals. In fact, rumour had it, he had started work in a butcher's shop!

"You see, Royston," Mr Gomersall had explained, "Buster tends to bite things that move. It's not really his fault. It's bred into him. It's part of his nature. He just can't help it. If those people had only stayed still, he wouldn't have gone for them."

The old man had got so upset about going into hospital and leaving Buster that Royston, on the spur of the moment, had volunteered to look after the dog.

"Are you sure your parents won't mind?" the old man had asked, brightening up.

"Oh no," Royston had assured him. "My mum and dad love dogs."

"Perhaps you should ask them, all the same," Mr Gomersall had suggested.

"No, no," replied Royston in a matter-of-fact voice. "They'll be fine, I know they will."

"Well, Royston!" exclaimed the old man. "You've lifted such a weight off my mind." He patted the fat round head of the dog that lay stretched out on the carpet beneath him. "Did you hear that, Buster? Young Royston here is going to look after you for a week or two. Now you be a good boy and don't go biting people."

The beast looked up and fixed Royston with its button eyes. They were as grey and as cold as an autumn sky. Buster growled his deep, low, throaty growl. As Royston stared down at the dog, he thought of the best way to induce his parents to let him look after Buster. This was going to need all his powers of persuasion.

"I'm sorry, Royston," Mrs Knapper was saying. Royston had given up on his dad and was tackling his mother, who was busy peeling potatoes at the kitchen sink. "We are not having the dog. You heard what your dad said. If it was up to me I'd probably say yes. I'd quite like a fluffy, friendly little dog to sit on my knee and stroke of an evening, but your dad has put his foot down, and that is that."

'Fluffy little dog to sit on her knee and stroke of an evening!' thought Royston. Fat chance of that. He could hardly picture Buster sitting on his mum's knee. Hanging by its teeth onto her neck like a vampire bat, yes, but sitting on her knee – hardly!

"Well, I'll pop round and let Mr Gomersall know the bad news then," Royston said sadly, "and tell him to make the final arrangements."

"What do you mean, the final arrangements?" asked Mrs Knapper, putting down a half-peeled potato. "I thought you said nobody would have the dog?"

"Nobody will," replied Royston, trying to make his voice wobble with emotion. "Mr Gomersall said that if no-one would look after Buster – and we were his very last hope – then he would have to have him put down."

"Put down?" repeated Royston's mum. "Do you mean put to sleep?"

"Killed!" said Royston bluntly. "Taken to the vet's and terminated."

"He can't do that!" cried Mrs Knapper.

"Mr Gomersall said Buster would just pine away if he was put in a kennel. He'd whine all day, wouldn't drink, wouldn't eat, he'd just waste away and die. It's the most humane solution to have him put down. Taking him to the vet's and having him put out of his misery is his only option now. Well, I hope that you and dad can live with yourselves."

"Oh, no, Royston, he can't have the dog put to sleep. There must be someone who would look after him," said Mrs Knapper, looking very concerned. "It would be inhuman to put the poor creature to sleep, that poor, frightened, affectionate little dog. I feel awful now."

"Well, if you and dad won't let me have him just for a measly week or two to help an unfortunate, lonely old man who's poorly as well and who has to go into hospital with his bad leg which he got fighting for his King and country in the War and who has no-one in the world except his true and faithful companion, then …"

"All right, all right, Royston, you don't need to rub salt

into the wound," said Mrs Knapper, drying her hands on the tea towel and wiping away a tear. "I'll have a word with your dad."

Sometimes, thought Royston, I excel myself, I truly do. That was such a brilliant performance. It deserved an award. "Oh, Mum," he said, patting her affectionately on the hand with the gentle expression of a serene angel. "Thanks."

And so it was that when Mr Gomersall left in the ambulance for the hospital, Royston took, or rather pulled and tugged, heaved and cajoled Buster home. When he dragged the fat snarling creature through the front door his mother froze.

"What," she exclaimed, "is that?"

"It's Buster," replied Royston, trying to sound cheerful.

"That, is Buster?" repeated Mrs Knapper, "Mr Gomersall's dog? That thing is Buster? That is the soft, affectionate, gentle, loveable little pooch that's going to sit on my knee?"

"You should never judge by appearances, Mum," Royston said. "That's what Mrs Gabbitas always says. 'It's not what's on the outside,' she always tells us, 'it's what's on the inside that matters.' 'You should never judge a book by its cover.' 'Beauty is only skin deep' and …"

"Royston!" snapped his mother. "Shut up!" She calmed down a little, and shook her head wearily. "You have a lot of explaining to do, young man. You led your father and me to believe that the dog would be no trouble."

"He won't," said Royston feebly.

"I can see trouble written all over that mean, malicious and cold-blooded face of his. He is walking trouble, that dog. I just know it."

Buster sniffed the air, puffed out his fleshy jowls, growled impressively and flopped on the hall carpet. Mrs Knapper went to close the door.

"Don't make any sudden movements, Mum," said Royston warily. "Buster tends to bite things that move."

"Wait until your father gets in, young man," said Mrs Knapper through gritted teeth, before retreating into the kitchen. "Just you wait until your father gets in."

When Mr Knapper set eyes on the dog he froze too,

and was, for once in his life, speechless. He stood at the door, staring at Buster without a word, his mouth gaping, and eyes like saucers.

"Say 'Hello', to Dad, Buster," said Royston, trying to put a brave face on it.

Buster sniffed the air, puffed out his fleshy jowls, growled impressively and raised himself on his stumpy legs.

"I shall be in the garage," Mr Knapper announced, suppressing his fury. "And I may be some time."

Buster soon made himself very much at home. By day, he basked lazily in the sunshine, sprawled on the front path, watching and waiting for any movement. By night, he reclined lazily in front of the fire, stretched on the carpet, watching and waiting for any movement. Buster tolerated Mrs Knapper and he put up with Royston, but he took a real shine to Mr Knapper. Royston was fascinated by the way the dog reacted to his father. Every time his dad entered the room, the dog would raise itself on its stumpy legs, wag its little sausage tail and nuzzle its fat face against him. The more Mr Knapper ignored it, the more the dog sought his attention. If Royston or his mum made a move to pat the stocky body or stroke the fat round head, Buster would growl ominously; it only had eyes for Mr Knapper.

"He really likes you, Dad," announced Royston at the breakfast table, the third day after Buster's arrival.

"He might like me," grumbled his father, "but I do not like him. He is, without doubt, the laziest, ugliest, grumpiest, most disagreeable mutt it has ever been my misfortune to meet. Just look at that face. He looks like he's walked into a door."

As if hearing his name called, the subject of the discussion trotted into the kitchen wagging its tail, and began nuzzling up to Mr Knapper.

"Go on Dad, give him a little pat," urged Royston.

"I'll give you a pat in a minute," replied his father, bristling. "And it won't be a little one."

Things had gone really well in the Knapper household that first week. Buster had not been any bother at all. When

Mrs Knapper called 'Breakfast!' up the stairs, the dog would appear at the kitchen door. He would then proceed to his bowls where he polished off half a pint of fresh creamy milk and ate a substantial meal of biscuits and meat. He would lick his chops, first one way and then the other, grunt with contentment, head for the front door and wait to be let out. For the remainder of the day he lay on the path sunning himself, waiting and watching until it was time for tea.

On Friday evening, when Royston and his father were watching a football match on the television, Mrs Knapper took up her needles as usual and smiled. She was knitting a jumper for Mr Knapper in the wildest of colours. He had several of the multicoloured monstrosities in his wardrobe, which had never seen the light of day. This was another creation that would remain unworn. Once, Mr Knapper had taken a whole caseful of jumpers down to the local charity shop, but the very apologetic lady had refused to accept them.

"You know, since this dog's been here," said Mrs Knapper, clacking away with the needles, "not one of those irritating door-to-door salesman has called."

"Oh yes," grunted Mr Knapper, his eyes glued to the television screen.

"And those dreadful politicians, who are forever canvassing for your vote and disturbing you, well they haven't called either."

"Oh yes," repeated Mr Knapper, not really listening.

"And those people who try to convert you to one religion or another. They haven't been around lately."

"Oh yes."

"It's so peaceful now. You could hear a pin drop."

It was true that since Buster's arrival no-one had visited the house and it was wonderfully quiet. The milkman had ceased clinking his bottles, the window cleaner had stopped his noisy singing, the paper boy had refrained from whistling and even the birds had remained silent. The ginger tomcat which invariably kept Mr and Mrs Knapper awake at night, moaning and meowing amorously, had not been seen since Buster came to stay.

"No," sighed Mrs Knapper. "It's been quite tranquil."

"Doris, I'm trying to watch the football here," complained her husband. "Could we have a bit of hush, do you think, please?"

Buster rolled over on his back and stuck his legs in the air, as if acknowledging the praise which was being lavished upon him by Royston's mother.

"And you know," continued Mrs Knapper, looking at Buster, "I'm getting used to him. He's quite cute really."

"Cute," laughed Mr Knapper, hollowly. "Did you say

cute? Ha! He's like a cross between a beer barrel and a
crocodile. He's about as cute as a werewolf when there's a
full moon, as cute as a tarantula down your underpants, as
cute as a starving shark in a swimming bath. That's how
cute he is." Buster, as if on cue, struggled to his feet,
lumbered over to Mr Knapper and rested his head on his
feet. "And another thing, what's all this about a poor,
defenceless animal pining away for its master? He misses
Mr Gomersall about as much as he'd miss a bad dose of
toothache, or a boil on his bottom."

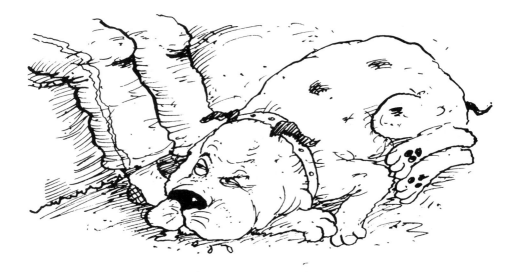

Royston noticed that his father had stopped pushing the
dog away now, and let Buster continue to rest his head on
his feet. He knew that secretly Mr Knapper was enjoying all
this attention, although he did not like to show it. Yes,
thought Royston, things had worked out really well.
But things did not continue like that for long.
On the Saturday morning, Buster ate a hearty breakfast

as usual and disappeared to take up his position on the path.
It was mid-morning when Mr Knapper thought he would
finish working on the engine of his car, and he set off for the
garage. Royston and his mother were in the kitchen at the
time, when they heard the most dreadful scream-cum-shriek-
cum-shout-cum-howl. It sounded like: Aaaaaahhhhhhggggggg!

Royston and his mum flew to the door to find
Mr Knapper staring in disbelief at Buster. The dog was
lying prone on the path, with a black and white rabbit
stuffed in its mouth.

"He's got a rabbit! He's got a rabbit!" shouted
Mr Knapper, jumping up and down.

"Oh my goodness!" cried Mrs Knapper.

Royston's father gripped the thick leather collar with
the silver studs which circled the dog's neck. He shook it
vigorously.

"Drop!" he commanded. "Drop, do you hear?"
The dog looked up with its cold grey button eyes, and

tightened its grip on the rabbit. "I said drop, you vicious, ugly, venomous cur!" shouted Mr Knapper. "This instant, do you hear me? Drop that rabbit!"

"Dad, it's not dropping it," wailed Royston

"I can see that!" his father snapped. " I don't need you to tell me the blindingly obvious." He turned his attention back to Buster. "Drop it!" he commanded again, but to no avail.

"What are you going to do?" asked Mrs Knapper in a frail voice.

"Doris, I do not know what I am going to do! What do you suggest I do? It won't open its mouth."

Royston's dad tried everything. He dangled a juicy morsel of meat before the grey eyes, he tapped the dog's fat head with a hairbrush, he even tried prising open the jaws with a spoon, but Buster resolutely held on to his victim.

"Right!" announced Mr Knapper. "I shall have to take it to the vet's. And you, young man," he said to Royston, stabbing the air with his finger in his son's direction, "are coming with me."

The journey through town was memorable. Buster stared with impassive curiosity from the back seat of the car, the rabbit still firmly wedged in his jaws. He caused quite a stir when drivers and pedestrians caught sight of him. In fact, there was very nearly an accident at the traffic lights when an astounded cyclist, catching sight of him sitting there, nearly fell off his bicycle in front of an oncoming bus.

The waiting room at the vet's was hot, packed and noisy. On the wooden benches that lined the walls, people and their pets were crammed shoulder to shoulder. There was an elderly lady with a great fluffy mass of white fur on her lap, a man holding a squawking parrot with a bald head, a little girl with a gerbil in a small wire cage, a boy with a hamster in a box, a woman with a goldfish in a bowl and more. When Royston's father entered carrying the dog (and attached rabbit) there was an audible intake of breath, then the room fell into an eerie silence. Buster growled his low throaty growl and let his glittery grey eyes sweep across the sea of terrified faces.

"Don't make any sudden moves," warned Mr Knapper, to no-one in particular. "He tends to bite anything that moves." People and their pets froze.

A cheerful, young receptionist in a pristine white overall entered. "Who's next?" she asked pleasantly.

"Him!" everyone chorused, pointing at Mr Knapper.

The vet, a plump, jovial man whose face was lost in a ridiculous red beard, placed Buster on his examination table and stared intently at him. "My goodness, he's a fine, healthy-looking specimen," he told Royston's dad, smiling widely. "Solid legs, good well-formed head, rounded rear, alert ears, wet nose, clear eyes. Yes, he's a fine animal. Is he a show dog?"

"It might have escaped your notice," said Royston's father irritably, ignoring the vet's question, "but the dog has a rabbit in its mouth."

"Yes, I can see that," the vet replied casually and then, after a moment, added, "It's dead."

"I know it's dead!" said Mr Knapper with mounting impatience. "I can see that it is dead." Two angry red spots appeared on his cheeks and it was with some difficulty that he controlled himself.

"Of course," said the vet, "when the dog picked the rabbit up it would have snapped its backbone like a nut."

"Oh dear, oh dear," moaned Royston's dad, a woeful expression passing over his face. He touched his perspiring brow with his fingertips.

"You see," continued the vet amiably, "this particular breed of dog has very, very powerful jaws. They are like clamps. Once locked, they are the devil's own job to open. Dogs, you know, have been domesticated for many hundreds of years, but they all still retain something of their killer instincts. It's part and parcel of their make-up, you see. They are descended from canine predators and even the most innocent-looking dog like a Chihuahua, a Miniature Poodle, or a Pekinese still have that urge to kill and that capability for attack."

Mr Knapper shot him a crushing glance. "Much as I would like to listen to the potted history of the canine world," he told him, his whole face now reddening with anger, "I want to know what you propose to do about the rabbit?"

"Well, not a lot," replied the vet. "As I said, it's dead. I'm not a miracle worker. I can't bring the rabbit back to life."

"I don't expect you to bring it back to life," growled Royston's father. "I can see that the rabbit is dead. It's not exactly jumping around is it? What I want is for you to remove it, to get it out of the dog's jaws, to extract it. The dog can't very well go through the rest of its life with a rabbit stuffed in its mouth, now can it?"

"Oh, I see," smiled the vet, unperturbed by the outburst. "Well, that shouldn't present too big a problem."

"Oh really?" said Royston's dad, giving a cynical smile. "You don't know Buster like I know Buster."

The vet stared into the animal's grey button eyes. The dog stared back coldly. "Now then old chap, what about letting me have the rabbit, eh?" Buster rumbled ominously. It was a deeply frightening sound. "Now then, now then," said the vet, apparently unconcerned. "Don't be so bad-tempered." He was either very brave or just plain stupid, thought Royston, as he watched him pat the fat body, and then take to stroking the dog behind the ears. To Royston's surprise, the deep growl miraculously changed into a sort of whimper, a kind of contented whining noise. "They like that," the vet told a fascinated Royston and a glowering Mr Knapper. Then Buster yawned, displaying a huge set of tank traps, and the rabbit flopped out onto the table.

"There we are," said the vet, picking up the rabbit and examining it. "Oh yes, it's been dead for some time. It's beginning to smell. It won't have felt a thing, of course,

when it was grabbed, if that's any consolation to you. Is it your rabbit, son?" asked the vet, looking in Royston's direction.

"No," Royston replied quietly. "It's not mine." This was not the time nor the place, he thought to himself, to say very much. Best keep a very low profile.

The vet, turning his attention back to Mr Knapper, asked genially, "Would you like me to put it in a box for you to take home?"

"The dog?" asked Royston's father with a curl of his lip. "That sounds an excellent idea."

"No, no," chuckled the vet. "The rabbit."

"No," said Mr Knapper, "I would not."

Royston's father settled the bill, an exorbitant amount to his way of thinking, for just tickling the dog. He carried Buster through the waiting-room to the car. The people on the benches clutched their frightened pets protectively as the dog eyed them with a wild sort of gleam in its little glittery eyes.

"Right, young man," said Mr Knapper when they were home. "I want you to get round to that hospital this minute and tell Mr Gomersall to make other arrangements. That dog has got to go."

"But, Dad …." started Royston.

"Don't 'But, Dad' me! Off you go and tell him that we are no longer having this… this … creature in the house for another moment."

"But, Dad …." Royston began again.

"Now!" snapped his father.

"And somebody will have to go around to Mrs Wood to tell her that her Tracey's rabbit has been killed," said Mrs Knapper, appearing at the door.

"What?" snapped her husband.

"I said someone will have to go around to Mrs Wood to tell …"

"I heard you! I heard you the first time!" shouted Mr Knapper. "What's all this about Tracey?"

"Well, it's her rabbit that Buster killed," explained Mrs Knapper.

"How do you know that?" demanded her husband.

"Because I recognised it. It's Bobby, that's what she called it. I used to see it every Saturday morning on my way to the shops. She put it out on the front lawn for a bit of exercise. I remember seeing it wandering about. That's when Buster must have seen it and …well, we all know the rest, don't we?"

"Well, you'll have to call round, Doris, and tell them," announced Mr Knapper.

"Me?" exclaimed his wife. "Why me?"

"Because I've been the one to take the monster to the

vet's, that's why, and I am certainly not trusting Royston to break the sad news. He'll only make things worse as he usually does. He's at the bottom of all this trouble, as always. I don't know why I was persuaded to take in that creature in the first place. I just knew something like this would happen. Now, you get off to the hospital, Royston, and tell Mr Gomersall he has to have his dog back, and your mother will go and tell Mrs Wood that the rabbit is dead."

Mr Gomersall was propped up when Royston arrived at his bedside. "Hello, Royston," said the old man cheerfully. "Lovely to see you. How's Buster?"

"Oh, he's – " Royston struggled for the right word to use – "all right."

"Missing me, I bet?"

"Yes, very much," he replied tactfully.

"Is he eating?"

"Yes, he's eating all right."

"And behaving himself?"

"Mr Gomersall…" began Royston, "…er…there's something I have to tell you and…"

The old man was clearly not listening. "Well, I've had my operation. I'm feeling fighting fit and I get out of hospital tomorrow.'

Great, thought Royston, all his troubles were at an end. He'd deliver Buster back, safe and sound, the very next day and that would be the end of the matter. But his heart sank when Mr Gomersall continued. "But there is a bit of a problem. You see, Royston, when I get home I have to take things easy for a while and there will be visits from the doctor, the community nurse, the health visitor and a home help that they are arranging for me. So you see my problem."

"Buster," said Royston quietly.

"I just can't have Buster back at the moment. What with all these visitors coming and going he would be disorientated and would end up biting them. I know he would, that's if they ever managed to get down the garden path in the first place. But it should be all right for him to come back in another couple of weeks or so."

"Another couple of weeks or so!" cried Royston.

"It will be all right for you to keep him until then, won't it?" said the old man. "He seems to be doing really well and is quite settled from what you said."

"Oh, he's quite settled all right," said Royston under his breath.

"So you'll keep Buster for another couple of weeks then?"

Royston hadn't the heart to say no. He'd have to think of a really, really good story to tell his father, something so convincing that they would have to keep the dog.

"Yes, of course," he replied. "We'd love to keep him."

All the way home Royston thought of some wild and wonderful reasons but he knew none would convince his mother, never mind his father, to keep the killer dog. He trudged slowly down the garden path, past the sprawling animal and through the front door.

"Is that you, Royston?" came a voice from the living room. It was Mr Knapper.

"Yes," replied Royston. His heart sank down into his trainers. What was he going to say?

His father appeared at the door. "Did you tell Mr Gomersall that we couldn't keep his dog?" he asked.

"Look, Dad I tried …" stammered Royston.

"Did you tell him?"

"I tried to tell him, honestly I did, but I ….

"Royston!" shouted his father. "Did you tell him?"

"No."

"Good," said his dad.

"Good?" repeated Royston. Had his dad gone mad? Had he been drinking? Had he had a message from another planet?

"The fact is, Royston," said his father, "that we've made a bit of a mistake. You see, your mother called at Mrs Wood's house to tell her about the rabbit and discovered that Buster hadn't killed it after all. In fact, the rabbit died of old age a couple of days ago. They found it dead in its hutch. They buried it in the garden beneath the old oak tree and Buster must have dug it up. So, he didn't kill it after all. I suppose it's a case of 'Give a dog a bad name…' "

"He didn't kill the rabbit then?" cried Royston.

"No, he didn't kill the rabbit," said his father.

"The only thing he was guilty of was digging it up."

"That's great, Dad," said Royston. "So we can keep Buster for a bit longer?"

"Yes, I suppose another couple of days is neither here nor there," replied his dad, giving one of his rare smiles.

"A couple of days?" repeated Royston, wondering how he was going to break the news that Buster might be spending Christmas with them!

Old Mouldybones

Mr Masterson, headteacher of Bogglesview School, smiled widely and warmly at the children sitting quietly in front of him. Next to him stood a tall stick of a man with rusty grey hair and a face like an old leather handbag, brown and blotchy and wrinkled. There was a little slit in the leather – a small obstinate mouth – and two glaring eyes, that glistened like chips of green glass.

"Will you all look this way, please," said Mr Masterson. "And that does include you, Royston Knapper, when you've quite finished your conversation with Timothy Joseph."

The wrinkled visitor glowered in the direction of the cheeky-faced boy with the mop of unruly hair and the face full of freckles.

Mr Masterson continued. "As you will all know by now, Mrs Gabbitas will be away for the rest of the month.

You will all be pleased to hear that she has had her operation and is well on the road to recovery. She wanted me to thank you all for the lovely cards, the flowers and best wishes. During Mrs Gabbitas's absence you will be having Mr Moulder-Jones as your teacher. He has very kindly volunteered to take your class until Mrs Gabbitas returns." The green eyes glistened and the little mouth twitched. "And I feel certain that the children will be on their very best behaviour, Mr Moulder-Jones."

"I know they will," said the new teacher. It was a low, eerie sort of a whisper which seemed to echo around the classroom. "I know they will," he repeated and gave a sickly smile.

"When I looked at my horoscope this morning," said Fozzy Foster to his friends as they made their way home, "it said that I was in for a shock today. It was spot on. And a right shock it was."

"Where did they dig up that 'Mouldybones' bloke from anyway?" asked Royston. "He's weird. He's straight out of a horror film. All he needs is a few dirty old bandages and he'd be the spitting image of the mummy in 'The Curse of the Pharaoh'."

"He used to teach my dad," said Timothy Joseph, filling his mouth with crisps and crunching noisily. "They rolled him out of retirement. They couldn't get anybody else at such short notice."

"Well, they want to roll him right back," moaned Fozzy. "He's horrible, really, really horrible. Those green eyes give me the creeps."

"And my dad says he's right strict," continued Timothy, spitting out bits of crisps as he spoke. "He used to teach games and P.E. and my dad said he made all the boys in his class run for miles in the thick snow, and play football in torrential rain, and play cricket in boiling hot weather with their jumpers on. My dad said that once he hit this lad over the head with a cricket stump just for whistling, and another time he made this lad stop in a freezing cold shower for half an hour, and another time he threw this big lump of chalk at this girl who was talking and it went up her nose and she had to go to hospital to have it taken out."

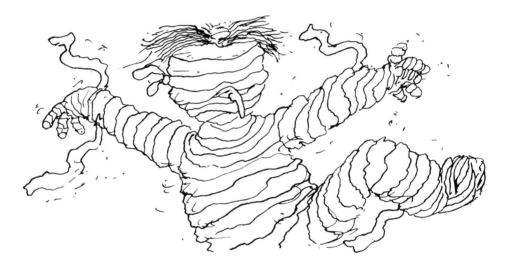

"He sounds really good fun," groaned Fozzy.

"He taught my dad to swim in one minute," said Timothy, ignoring the interruption. "He threw my dad in the deep end at the baths and told him to swim for it."

"It gets better," Fozzy sighed noisily.

"My dad says nobody messed around in old Jonesy's class. He said there ought to be more teachers around like him. He says kids have it too easy these days. A dose of good old-fashioned discipline is what's needed."

"I think your dad's been talking to mine," said Royston. "He sounds just like my dad."

"I shan't sleep a wink this weekend thinking about him," sighed Fozzy. "I'll have nightmares, I know I will. Fancy lumbering us with an antique teacher like old 'Mouldybones'. There ought to be a law against it."

On Monday morning Fozzy was still moaning and groaning about Mr Moulder-Jones.

"I think old 'Mouldybones' has a fan club. When I told my mum about him she said he taught my Uncle Brian and my Auntie Doreen, and she said that if there were more teachers like him there wouldn't be any football hooligans and muggers roaming the streets."

"They'd all probably be in hospital with cracked heads or pneumonia or heat rash or chalk up their noses," said Royston. "That seems to be the way he deals with people."

"Oh, stop going on about him," said Timothy, impatiently. "You've got him on the brain. He's probably not as bad as everybody thinks."

Timothy Joseph was wrong. Mr Moulder-Jones was everything Fozzy had dreaded – and more.

When the children arrived at their classroom that morning, they didn't recognise it. The nature table was bare, the stuffed animals and birds were pushed in a corner, the computer was packed away in its box, the wall displays had been replaced by a series of faded, dog-eared posters on 'Prepositions' and 'Verbs' and the desks had been moved into straight rows facing the front.

Mr Moulder-Jones was busy writing on the blackboard, very slowly and very carefully.

"What's everybody waiting for?" Royston asked Penelope Pringle. "Why don't you go in?"

"Nobody dare," she replied. "He once threw this piece of chalk at this girl and it …"

"Went up her nose," interrupted Royston. "I heard. Move out of the way and I'll ask if we can come in. We can't stay out here all day."

"More's the pity," came Fozzy's voice from the back of the queue.

Royston poked his head round the door. The wrinkled head turned slowly in his direction like a tortoise's and the green eyes glinted. "Sir, can we come in?" asked Royston cheerfully.

"You certainly can come in, but whether you may is another matter," came the reply.

"What's he say?" whispered Timothy Joseph into Royston's ear.

"I've no idea," replied Royston. "He said I can and

then he said I can't."

"Do you think he's gone a bit funny in the head?" asked Timothy, peering around the door. "Ask him again."

"Does that mean I can come in, Sir?" enquired Royston pleasantly.

"I shall inform you when you may come in," said Mr Moulder-Jones, and carried on writing. "Remain at the door in a quiet and orderly fashion."

Five minutes later the class was sitting motionless and silent, all eyes on the new teacher.

"You will have noticed," began Mr Moulder-Jones, "that the classroom is rather different. I have altered it to suit my way of teaching. I don't want any distractions – pictures and stuffed animals and plants and computers and the like. We are here to work, not to spend our time idly looking at fanciful displays. I took your books home this weekend to see the standard of work of this class." He paused and scanned the serious faces before him. "And I was far from impressed. Untidy scribble, spelling errors, grammatical mistakes. One book, in particular, looked as if a lot of drunken spiders had found their way into an ink-well and scuttled across the pages." Royston knew well to whom he was referring. "We will be spending a lot of time on handwriting. We will also be doing something about the atrocious spelling. Where is the boy Foster?"

Fozzy's face, which was naturally pale, turned even paler. Then he raised a trembling hand.

"Your work is completely indecipherable, Foster. It's like some sort of code to deceive the enemy. There are full stops and flying commas, question marks and dashes all over the place and I've not the slightest idea about what you are

writing. What is an E-G-O-G?"

"It's an 'edgehog, Sir," replied Fozzy.

"You will spend break and lunchtime writing out all the corrected spellings ten times. I do not know what Mrs Gabbitas has been doing with you in this class, but she has certainly done little about the presentation and the accuracy of your work. Far too much airy-fairy poetry and story writing. But I shall soon remedy that. Where is the girl, Penelope Pringle?"

Penelope raised her hand and gave a weak smile. If she expected the sort of praise Mrs Gabbitas was wont to lavish upon her, she was soon made aware of her mistake. Mr Moulder-Jones held up her book. She waited for him to say, 'This is the sort of work I want,' but it was not forthcoming. "What is this?" he snapped.

"What, Sir?" she asked in her usual confident tone of voice.

"All these fancy doodles and drawings in the margin and at the end of your work."

"They're my illustrations, Sir," she replied, rather peeved. "They make my writing more interesting and colourful." Then she added for good measure, "Mrs Gabbitas likes them."

"Well, I do not, so don't do them again."

"But, Sir ...." she began.

"Excuse me?" said Mr Moulder-Jones.

"I was just going to say ..." Penelope started again.

"Excuse me?" repeated the teacher, fixing her with an icy glare. "I think that is the end of the discussion."

Penelope pouted and looked down angrily.

"Where's the boy who so rudely interrupted me this morning?"

"Me, Sir," said Royston, waving his hand in the air like a daffodil in the wind.

"When you raise your hand keep it straight; you are not hailing a taxi. And take that silly smile off your face. What is the difference between the words 'can' and 'may'?"

Royston flicked the hair out of his eyes and stuck his tongue theatrically in the corner of his mouth, his face fierce with concentration.

"Come on! Come on! Spit it out. We haven't got all day!"

"Sir, a 'can' is what beans come in, and 'May' is a month."

Mr Moulder-Jones breathed in heavily through flared nostrils and his eyes became slits. "I hope you are not trying to be insolent."

"No, Sir," replied Royston in the most innocent of voices.

"The word 'can' is an auxiliary verb expressing an ability or knowledge of how to do something, as in the sentence: 'I can throw this piece of chalk'." All the children covered their noses. "The word 'may' is another auxiliary verb expressing the possibility or the permission to do something, as in the sentence: 'You may enter the room.' Is that clear?"

About as clear as mud, thought Royston. "Oh yes, Sir," he replied. "Perfectly clear."

"So when you ask: 'Can I enter the room?' of course you can, you are able to enter, you have the ability to enter, you have the legs to carry you into the room, but that is a different matter from whether you have permission and may enter. You will spend morning break writing out the chapter entitled: 'Parts of the Verb' from this book." He held up the oldest, dirtiest, dustiest book Royston had ever seen.

Everyone remained in at break, writing out spellings, copying from books, doing extra maths or practising handwriting. Even Penelope Pringle and Nassim Pervez, the best writers in the class, had to stay in.

"I thought Mrs Gabbitas was bad enough," complained Fozzy at the dinner table, "rambling on and on, but she's got nothing on old 'Mouldybones'. He's horrible, really, really horrible."

"It's like being in prison," sighed Timothy. "Stand up straight, keep quiet, do this, don't do that. He made me copy that work from the board three times and then he tore it up and threw it in the bin."

"He's quite put me off my sandwiches," said Fozzy.

If the morning was bad, the afternoon was worse. It started with mental arithmetic. Mr Moulder-Jones fired questions in every direction like a machine gun and those who answered incorrectly were made to stand on their chairs. Even Simon Morgan and Audrey Jaworski, who were best in maths, ended up with the rest, two feet off the ground.

"I don't know what Mrs Gabbitas has been doing with you in this class but she has certainly not done much arithmetic," said Mr Moulder-Jones in his rasping, eerie sort of voice, to no-one in particular. "All this airy-fairy, namby-pamby, write-what-you-want, do-as-you-like nonsense. I don't know what schools are coming to."

On the Tuesday morning it was a sad, quiet, grim-faced group of children that queued outside the classroom. Inside, Mr Moulder-Jones was busy at the blackboard. He motioned with a long bony finger for the class to enter and then returned to his slow, careful writing. As Royston passed the tall figure, two bony fingers and a thumb grabbed his ear.

"Are you whistling, boy?"

"Yes, Sir," replied Royston.

"Why are you whistling?"

"Sir, because I'm happy, Sir."

"You have no business to be happy. You are here at school to learn, to work hard and behave yourself, not to whistle and be happy. Birds whistle, human beings are blessed with the ability to speak." Chance would be a fine thing, thought Royston. The only person who had spoken yesterday was old 'Mouldybones' himself. Everybody else had been too scared to open their mouths. "You will remain in this room at break and write out a hundred times: 'I would be better occupied learning my tables than imitating the activities of feathered creatures.' Now sit down and shut up." The little green eyes flashed in the direction of Fozzy, who was scratching his head thoughtfully. "What are you doing, boy?" demanded Mr Moulder-Jones.

"Nnnnnnothing, sir," stuttered Fozzy.

"Exactly. Nothing. You would be well advised, Foster, to learn those spellings you copied out yesterday, instead of scratching your scalp. I have my doubts whether there's anything inside that head of yours." There was a little grin of satisfaction on the small mouth.

"Sir, I was going to, Sir, I was just sat here wondering where I'd put my book, Sir."

"I was just sat here! I was just sat here!" repeated Mr Moulder-Jones. "You were not just sat there, Foster, you were sitting there. I sit (present tense), yesterday I sat (past tense), I am sitting (present participle). Do you understand?"

"No, Sir," replied Fozzy in a feeble voice.

"Why don't you understand? It's quite a simple concept: I sit, I sat, I am sitting!"

"But you're not sitting, Sir, you're stood."

"I know I am stood…I mean standing!" snapped Mr Moulder-Jones.

Fozzy was getting more and more red and flustered and confused, as indeed were all the rest of the children, who avoided looking in the direction of the little green eyes in case they settled on them.

"Remain here at morning break, Foster, and copy out the chapter: 'The Correct Usage of the Verb' from this book. You will then learn it and tomorrow I will test you." Mr Moulder-Jones held up the dirty, dusty old book Royston had used the day before.

For the rest of the morning the class listened to a boring, endless monologue from Mr Moulder-Jones about 'The Language of Animals': how ants rub their antennae together, how bees buzz information to each other, how frogs croak their feelings and serpents hiss their anger.

"And so," concluded Mr Moulder-Jones, "animals are only able to convey expressions of hunger, impatience, anger and fear, but such sounds cannot be considered as language. Only human beings can use language. And since we have the gift of language, Royston Knapper, we should use it, not go around whistling like a half-strangled starling." Mr Moulder-Jones paused fractionally and smiled at his clever remark. "Tomorrow you will all have a test on this subject, so I hope you have been concentrating on what I have said."

At lunchtime, Fozzy turned on Royston. "If you hadn't come in whistling we wouldn't have had to listen to all that boring stuff about animals."

"And we have to remember it all for a test tomorrow," complained Timothy.

"Don't blame me," said Royston. "All I did was whistle."

"He's horrible, really, really horrible," said Fozzy, screwing up his face. "He thinks he's so clever with his: 'I have doubts whether there's anything inside that head of yours,' and his: 'You'd be well advised to learn your

spellings,' and his: 'You are here to learn, not to whistle.'
He can go and whistle. He's horrible and he's always saying
nasty things about Mrs Gabbitas as well. I'd have her
instead of him any day and I'd write soppy poetry. At least
she let us talk and we did interesting things, and we went to
places and she wasn't sarcastic all the time."

"Well, what are we going to do?" asked Timothy.

"I wish I could be ill for the rest of the month," Fozzy
told them.

"We'll have to fix him," said Royston. "Now listen
carefully, and I'll explain what I have in mind."

Wednesday morning arrived and the class queued
quietly outside the classroom awaiting the signal from
Mr Moulder-Jones to enter. He was adding the finishing
touches to a long set of questions on the blackboard. Then
long bony fingers gestured to Rajvir Singh, who was at the
front of the queue, and the children filed in silently.

Mr Moulder-Jones rubbed his long hands together to
remove the chalk dust. He then steepled his fingers and

watched and waited, until everybody was seated and listening. Then he began.

"On the blackboard are twenty questions concerned with the work we did yesterday on 'The Language of Animals'. I want you to read them carefully and write down the answers in your books, remembering to take care with the spellings and the handwriting. Those of you who produce unsatisfactory work will remain in at break and re-write it."

He turned and gestured in the direction of the board. Then it happened. There was a faint buzzing noise near the back of the classroom. It sounded like a fly or a bee. Mr Moulder-Jones looked up. The buzzing got louder. The teacher's small eyes glinted. They shot this way and that. Then there was a sort of quack, then a whistle, and a moo, and a cluck.

There was a deathly silence. Mr Moulder-Jones's little green eyes flashed fiercely and his mouth twitched. He didn't know what to do.

"Who is it making those silly noises?" His voice was trembling with anger. "Who is it? Stand up the idiot who thinks this classroom is a farmyard."

Nobody moved, nobody spoke. The buzzing started again. This was followed by whistling, mooing, clucking, barking, quacking, hooting, grunting, snorting, growling – every conceivable animal noise. Soon everybody in the class was joining in and the babble increased in volume and variety.

"Stop it! Stop it, I say! Stop it at once!" roared Mr Moulder-Jones. He banged the flat of his hand on the desk top. "Do you hear me?" he screamed. His voice now

sounded high-pitched and panicky. He began rushing up and down the rows, shouting and shrieking and telling everybody to be quiet.

The noise suddenly stopped. Mr Masterson stood at the door, a look of amazement on his face. Behind him stood Mrs Quinn, the school secretary, with a terrified expression on hers. The headteacher stared first at the children, then turned to Mr Moulder-Jones, who was by now sitting on his chair breathing heavily, his wrinkled head bent so low that his chin rested on his chest.

"Whatever is happening?" Mr Masterson demanded. Mr Moulder-Jones raised his head, but before he could open his mouth, Royston answered.

"Sir, it's the language of animals, Sir. We've been learning about it with Mr Moulder-Jones, Sir."

"We were having a test on it, Sir," added Penelope.

"Oh, really! Is that what's going on?" said Mr Masterson, sounding totally unconvinced. "Well do it quietly. I'm trying to work down the corridor. Mrs Quinn thought that a herd of wild animals had got into school." The school secretary nodded vigorously in agreement. "Don't let me have to come into this room again, or there'll be trouble." He gave Mr Moulder-Jones a peculiar sort of look and disappeared down the corridor, leaving the classroom door open.

Old 'Mouldybones' wasn't seen again in Bogglesview School. Times had changed and teachers could no longer scare children by hitting them and making sarcastic comments. Mr Moulder-Jones knew he would never go into a classroom again. It was the end of an era.

"He must have been a bit past it," said Fozzy's dad when he heard. "Oooo, but he was a strict teacher. Nobody messed around in old Jonesy's class, I can tell you. Your Uncle Brian still bears the scars and your Auntie Doreen quivers at the mere mention of his name. I remember once he threw this piece of chalk at Irene Clamp and…"

"I know, Dad, you've told me hundreds of times," replied Fozzy.

Royston and Penelope were the first to go and see Mrs Gabbitas on her return to school. The children hovered outside the door, uncertain whether or not to enter.

"May we come in, Miss?" asked Penelope Pringle in a shy little voice.

"Of course. Come in, come in," shouted Mrs Gabbitas. "You don't need to stand out there. It's lovely to see you."

The classroom was back to normal. The nature table was full of conkers and nuts, shells and dried flowers; the computer hummed in the corner; bright posters covered the walls; the stuffed animals were back in place, and the desks had been pushed together to form tables.

"I'm so glad to be back," said the teacher. "My goodness, I've missed everyone."

"We've missed you as well, Miss," said Royston.

"I beg your pardon, Royston Knapper?" gasped the teacher.

"I said we've all missed you, Miss. It's good to have you back."

"It is, Miss," echoed Penelope.

"Well, I'm completely lost for words," said Mrs Gabbitas. "I'd never thought I'd hear you say that, Royston Knapper. You know, when you want to be, you can be a very nice boy. Now what about giving me a hand?"

"Yes, Miss," replied Royston cheerfully.

"Would you put a book on each desk please? I thought I'd start with one of my favourite stories this morning. I'm sure everyone will enjoy it as much as I do. It's about

a really unusual and amusing man called Doctor Dolittle, who can talk to animals. Not many people know this, you know, but all animals have a language of their own. Fascinating isn't it?"

You could have heard a pin drop. "Well, what is it Royston?" said Mrs Gabbitas. "You look as if the cat's got your tongue."